Also By Pa

Goose and
Slings and Sparrows

Spokane Clock Tower Mysteries
Butcher, Baker, Candlestick Taker
Cupboards All Bared
Crazy Maids in a Row

Anna Katharine Green Mysteries
A Deed of Dreadful Note

Sam Shovel Mysteries
Death of a Christmas Tree Salesman

Poetry and Short Stories
Happenings
Murder for a Jar of Red Rum

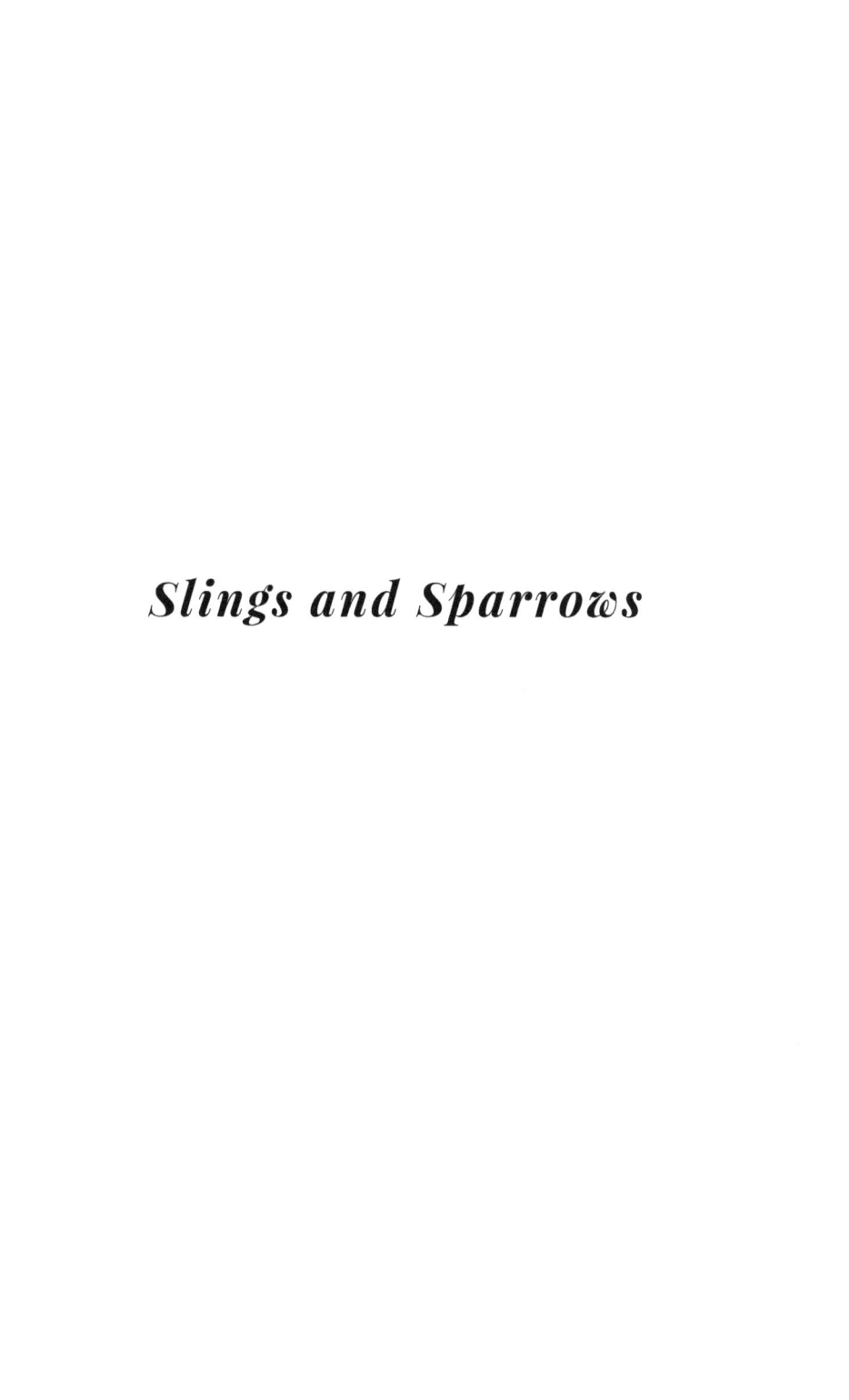

Slings and Sparrows

Slings and Sparrows

A Goose and Penny Mystery

Patricia Meredith

Games Afoot, LLC

Copyright © 2024 by Patricia Meredith

All rights reserved. No part of this book may be reproduced in any manner whatsoever without written permission except in the case of brief quotations embodied in critical articles and reviews.

Cover art and design by Patricia Meredith

First Printing, 2024

This book is dedicated to Linda and Mike Chase,
who welcomed me onto their farm and
into the loving embrace of every peacock, chicken,
duck, quail, and guinea fowl on the place.

"Who killed Cock Robin?
I, said the Sparrow,
with my bow and arrow,
I killed Cock Robin."

—"Death of Cock Robin," *Tommy Thumb's Pretty Song Book*

"Whether 'tis nobler in the mind to suffer the slings
and arrows of outrageous fortune,
Or to take arms against a sea of troubles,
and by opposing end them."

—William Shakespeare, *Hamlet*

The Old Bird Society

(IN ORDER OF MEMBERSHIP)

Gertrude "Goose" Fulton — Sister of Penny, retired Victorian Literature professor

    Geese: Tomi and Tuppence

Penelope "Penny" Wilcox — Sister of Goose, cataloger at the Paca Springs Museum

    Chicken: Henny

Constance "Connie" Wilcox — Aunt to Goose and Penny, owner of the Quaint Quail Café

    Quail

Beatrice Johnson — Costume designer

    Peacocks

Mary "Sable" Amsel — Professor of agriculture

    Raven: Hugin

Alice Ledford — Psychiatrist

    Guinea fowl

Ruth Collingwood — Retired Army nurse

    Ducks

Maya Grove — Professional performer

    Cockatiel: Casper

{ 1 }

In Which Cock Robin Comes to an Untimely Demise

The day Cock Robin was murdered started like any other day, with the peacock crowing up the morning sun.

Yes, the *peacock*.

"You know," I said, "royalty used to consider peacock a delicacy. Perhaps it's about time we brought the custom back."

"Don't say such things!" my sister Penny cried, covering the ears of her comfort chicken, Henny, as though she might take offense.

So like I said, it was like any other day.

I didn't notice anything was wrong until it was too quiet during breakfast. I was sitting there, drinking my orange juice and eating my bagel, reading *The Paca Springs Gazette*, when I realized I could hear my own thoughts. They weren't being drowned out by the latest rendition of "Edelweiss" being whistled by—no, not by a canary, good guess—a cockatiel.

Our latest renter, Maya, had trained her cockatiel from a young age to sing, and he was good.

And boy, didn't he know it. Every time I saw him—the few brief times Maya let me peek at His Majesty before covering him up for his "beauty sleep"—he was usually standing there, his white feathered chest and red cheeks puffed up with his own perfection, his yellow-feathered mohawk sticking straight into the sky, his beady eyes glinting with his own excellence.

He was a regular Cock Robin, though Maya insisted he should be referred to by his professional stage name, Casper the Whistling Cockatiel. She said he was named after Casper Reardon, a famous harpist. But I think most people's thoughts, like mine, went directly to the cartoon "friendly ghost."

Which he'd just become, apparently, as Maya came running in, her dyed brown hair with ombre bronze highlights a strangled mess, yelling, "Someone's killed Casper!"

Maya had what we Victorian literature professors might describe as a Rubenesque figure, meaning even at sixty, she had curves in all the right places. This might have made some people dislike her from the start. She was really quite sweet, though you wouldn't have known it to look at her now: her tan cheeks were flushed with anger.

I slowly set down the paper, folding it in half to hide the story I'd been reading—a rather disturbing report about some famous boxer named Mike Tyson who had just been banned for biting someone's ear off. Nevertheless, whatever Maya was on about sounded a lot more interesting.

"Killed? That's a bit of a jump. I'm sure he just died in his sleep," I said.

"Why would you say that? You must have killed him!"

"Me?"

"Yes. I know you never liked him."

"Now, Maya," Penny said softly, her grip on Henny tightening enough to make her give a small cluck. "I'm certain no one has killed Casper. Least of all Goose. She'd never hurt a flea."

I nodded in affirmation. "I would never kill a bird. Not even for Thanksgiving." I took a sip of orange juice. "And I'm still confused why you're convinced someone killed him. What makes you think he didn't die of natural causes?"

"He has an arrow through his breast."

"What?!" I jumped up and pushed past Maya to the sunroom where Casper had his own private birdhouse along the south wall.

I nearly bit my lip in shock when I saw she was right. Someone had pierced Casper with something long and sharp, right through his chest. I looked about for something the weapon might have come from, some bit of a tomato cage or a loose part of his own birdcage. But nothing around him was missing a thin, sharp fragment that could pierce a cockatiel through.

He lay in the bottom of his cage, his little feet curled as though still clinging to his perch, his beak pointing straight up at the sky.

It was honestly a rather terrible sight.

My sister stood on the other side of me, paler than usual and covering Henny's eyes.

I came in close and opened the door to his cage slowly.

"Please, let me," Maya said, pushing me aside.

She reached through the opening and gently removed the body.

"My poor, sweet Casper," Maya cried, her eyes welling up with tears. "Who would do such a thing? *Why* would someone do such a thing?" she asked accusatorially, as though one of us had done this senseless act.

She turned, carried Casper to a chair, and sat down, cradling his broken body in her palm. My sister and I watched reverently as Maya pulled the sharp fragment smoothly out of his body and held it up.

It was a hatpin about six inches long. At that length, it would normally be used for decorating a hat, unlike the ten-inch ones which were used for holding a hat to the wearer's head. Only someone of our generation would realize the difference, or someone fascinated by a bygone era when hatpins were used regularly.

I looked from the pin to Maya and back again.

"I knew it," she murmured. "Beatrice."

I hadn't wanted to say it myself, but I only knew one person who used pins like that. Beatrice used them to pin her decorative peacock feathers to the hats she sold at craft fairs and farmers markets. She also made earrings, necklaces, brooches, pens, hair barrettes, and more from the long, luxurious feathers her birds molted every summer.

"Beatrice would never hurt a bird," I said defensively. "None of the OBS ladies would."

The fact was, we were all too fond of birds and knew what it would be like if someone hurt ours, so we'd never think of hurting someone else's. It was our fondness for our feathered friends that had caused my sister and I to turn our land on the PA side of Maryland's narrow waist into the OBS in the first place.

It started with Penny and me, Goose. Penny had called me "Goose" since we were children, I think because my favorite book to read to her was a collection of Mother Goose rhymes. Plus, I tended to mother her a bit. It wasn't my fault. I couldn't help myself. Our mother died when we were three and five years old, so someone had to step in to the role. Of course it was the older sister.

Penny always needed help. She often struggled with feeling anxious—even these days, and we were in our sixties now. Although it became popular in the '50s for doctors to prescribe drugs, when we were growing up in the '40s it was more common to hear something akin to today's "suck it up, buttercup." I don't know why Dad came home with a hen one day, but Penny was fourteen and she'd had what I like to call a "comfort chicken" ever since. She always named them Henny, so together they were Henny Penny, like the *Chicken Little* character, forever on the lookout for the next piece of sky that might fall.

This most recent version of Henny loved being cuddled and carried under one arm. No purse or carrier for this chicken. She wanted to be nestled right up close to Penny. Henny was a silver-laced Cochin, a relatively new breed that had first appeared in the '60s and was still holding strong thirty years later. I wasn't surprised, seeing as she was the fluffiest, cutest chicken out there. She was quiet, too, not making a sound except to practically *purr* when she was happy with the attention she was getting.

I preferred geese. Loud, obnoxious, and in-your-face though they were, at least you knew what you were getting into when it came to them. I had two Embden geese named Tomi and Tuppence who waddled about gabbing all day long, sharing stories and thrilling tales of derring-do just like their namesakes. I absolutely adored the series of books by Agatha Christie featuring the original comedic detecting duo and their insanely witty banter.

Now, seeing our trend toward poultry, my Aunt Connie had decided it would be a good idea to send our way anyone who drank a pot of tea at her café who was about our age who owned a bird or two. After my friend Beatrice with her peacocks came Sable with her raven, Alice with her guinea fowl, and Ruth with her ducks, ranging in age from Alice in her late fifties to Ruth in her late sixties. Each gal rented a bit of land and a home somewhere on our sixty-seven acres, and they each came with a bird. So what else could we call ourselves but a bird sanctuary?

Course we couldn't call it "BS," so we called ourselves the "OBS" for "Old Bird Society."

Sure, one might argue for "Middle-Aged Birds" or "Birds of a Certain Age" but honestly, they just didn't have the same ring to them. The point was: we didn't mind laughing at ourselves once in a while and truth-be-told, we were a bunch of old birds with our birds. So there you go.

Slings and Sparrows

Maya was our newest addition with Casper. While they were building her home, she was renting a room with us. Naturally, Casper moved in, too.

You'd think I'd have built up a tolerance for bird sounds, from Tomi and Tuppence's constant gabbling to the peacocks yelping like car alarms whenever someone approached. I honestly hadn't realized a professional whistling bird would get on my nerves so quickly. Three weeks in and I was ready to kill the bird myself.

But I didn't. I wasn't sure who did, but I intended to find out.

"It must have been an accident," Penny murmured softly behind me, running an agitated hand over Henny's back feathers.

Maya glared at the pair of them.

"You're saying one of Beatrice's hatpins *accidentally* impaled him?"

"Well, when you put it that way," Penny said so quietly only I heard her.

"No more accusations or assumptions," I declared, taking control. "There's nothing to be done. Casper is dead. It's sad, but true."

Maya's face went bright red as she rose from her chair.

"Someone will pay for this," she growled.

With a flutter, she left the room, the tiny broken body cradled in her hands.

{ 2 }

In Which We're On Pins and Needles

"Well, Penny, looks like you got your wish."

I sidled up and wrapped an arm around Penny, Henny burping a soft cluck as she was sandwiched between us.

"I never wished for Casper to die," she half whispered.

"Meh, perhaps not aloud, but I know in your heart of hearts waking up to sliding vocal warm-ups was starting to bother even you." I looked down at the top of Henny's head. "Or at least Henny. But no, what I meant was: you finally have your own personal murder mystery to solve!"

Penny glanced at me out of the corner of her eye. I could tell she was fighting the fact that I was right, as usual. There are some things sisters never grow out of.

"I'd rather not get excited about a murder," she said quietly, staring at the empty cage that had once held the professional songbird.

"Oh, come on. Even Sherlock admits he'd rather have a case to solve than 'die of stagnation.' And I'm pretty sure Poirot gets happy every time someone attempts to outwit his 'little gray cells.'" I gave my best attempt at a Belgian accent.

Penny wasn't the only one who enjoyed a good detective novel. I loved an evening curled up with a good Golden Age mystery just as much as she did, though lately I found myself drawn more to Anna Katharine Green and Wilkie Collins, and the early detective stories that inspired authors like Agatha Christie, G.K. Chesterton, and Dorothy L. Sayers.

I, therefore, had a million other references I might have made to spur Penny on, but in the end I just said, "The point is: murder is terrible, but detection is fun."

I gave Penny's shoulders a squeeze again and let her go. I was done arguing and ready to move on, whether Penny decided to help me or not. I rubbed my hands together gleefully.

Penny frowned and ran a hand over Henny's back. Then she sighed. "Oh, all right," she said. "I suppose we should start with the facts. What can we learn from the scene of the crime?"

I gave the cage a good looking over. "There's no blood spatter. And no bird droppings on the newspaper covering the bottom, so that means the cage had been recently cleaned."

"I concur."

I gave a sniff. "Smells clean, too. The brass bars have a dull shine to them, though, so it's not a new cage."

"I'm almost certain this is the same cage Casper arrived in. Do you know how long Casper and Maya have been Casper and Maya?"

I shook my head. "Something to ask her later."

I looked closer at the bottom of the cage. "Odd," I said, but left my sister hanging like any book-worthy detective.

"What?" she asked, coming closer and trying to see what I'd seen.

I reached into the cage and picked up the two things I'd found, holding them out on my palm for Penny and Henny to see.

"More pins," Penny said.

I nodded. "But not hatpins. They're too small."

"I wonder what they were for?"

I looked back at the cage, at the perch, lifting my glasses so I could see clearly without the distraction of my bifocals.

"I see now why detectives use magnifying glasses," I muttered. I asked Penny to take a look for me. "Do you see anything on the perch? Any markings?"

Penny studied the wooden dowel. "Yes!" she said excitedly. "There are two small holes a couple inches apart."

I pointed to the bottom of the pins. "This size?"

"Yes. What does it mean, Goose?"

"It means: he's a dead parrot!"

"He's a *cockatiel*," Penny said with a confused look.

"Casper is no more, he has ceased to be, he is bereft of life, he rests in peace." I turned and looked Penny in the eyes. "He is an ex-cockatiel."

"Oh!" squeaked Penny, smiling at Henny as though wondering if she'd caught the reference, too. "I get it! The Monty Python sketch!"

I presented an open palm to her in congratulations. "Exactly."

Penny slapped my hand. "But...why? Why would someone nail this poor bird's feet to its perch?"

"To give them a non-moving target for shooting a hatpin?" I suggested.

Penny leaned over the pins in my palm again. "They look like mounting pins for insects or something." Henny clucked in agreement.

"Does anyone in the OBS collect butterflies?"

Penny bit her lip. "Not that I know of. But if I had to guess, I'd say Sable might."

Beatrice, Sable, and I had met in a Victorian Gothic literature class in college. It was while studying Poe, Shelley, Radcliffe, and the like we'd noticed Sable starting a trend toward wearing only black. In fact, she'd continued to do so even as a professor, possibly inspiring her students to follow in her dressing habits, and becoming the bellwether of the goth movement in the '80s. No matter what, I could always count on Sable for a fantastic discussion of the mysterious and the macabre.

"Now why would you say that?" I asked.

"Doesn't she seem like the type to pin helpless insects to a board for the good of scientific research?"

To be fair, Sable *was* a scientist, but her focus was on agriculture and horticulture. Unless she thought butterflies might tell her why her cabbage was covered in slugs, I didn't think she'd care to collect them.

"Where would she have space for such a hobby?" I countered. Sable lived in a tiny home—no more than two hundred square feet—with her raven. Her life was lived outside, so she had little use for indoor living and therefore little space for large boards full of pinned insects.

Penny shrugged. "That's true." Her hand was still methodically rubbing down the back of Henny. "Then perhaps Ruth?"

Ah, Ruth. Ruth was a retired Army nurse and she never let you forget it. She insisted that her flock of ducks were "battle-ready"—which sounded like a punchline until you talked to her. I once asked her if she thought a goose might join their ranks and she practically quacked in my face. Never suggested that again.

What all that had to do with butterfly pins, however, I wasn't too sure.

"She just seems like the more...aggressive type," Penny said tentatively. She glanced about, as though afraid Ruth had placed recording devices behind the potted plants filling the sunroom.

"What about Beatrice?" I asked. "After all, the larger pin looked to be one of hers. Perhaps she uses these smaller mounting pins for something costume-oriented, as well?"

Even as I said it I realized I may be on the right track, though I still couldn't imagine Beatrice in her voluminous Edwardian skirts getting so aggressive. But, then again, you'd never think a peacock would get aggressive either and then *wham!* One attacks the other and you learn even the prettiest bird in the world has a dark side.

"You're thinking about when Beatrice's peacock killed another male for going after his mate, aren't you?" Penny asked, no doubt reading the crease in my brow. We may not be twins, but it was eerie how often Penny read my mind.

Slings and Sparrows

I could still see Beatrice's tear-stained face as she'd held the wounded bird. The peacock who'd been killed was named Don Pedro, after the character in *Much Ado About Nothing*. He had been her third peacock. Her second peacock, Claudio, had gotten it into his head that Don Pedro was after his mate, Hero, and had continually attacked him. One day, he'd been successful. Interesting how their given names seemed to affect their fates.

Beatrice had cradled him in her arms, sobbing quietly, her mascara leaving black lines down her chestnut cheeks. It was the way of the bird world, but it was still difficult for some of us to accept. We were forever trying to anthropomorphize our animal friends, giving them aspects of our humanity. This was why I had a difficult time believing *any* of the ladies would have done such a horrible thing as murder another woman's bird.

I looked about for the long pin Maya had pulled from Casper. Penny held it out to me. I picked it up with a thankful smile and placed it next to the other two, much smaller pins. It wasn't a matched set, but how many pins were?

"I'm afraid we're going to have to question Beatrice," I said.

"*You're* going to have to question Beatrice," Penny clarified, with a glance at her wristwatch. "*I* have to get to work."

I waved her off with my empty hand. "Surely the museum can make it one day without their cataloger. It's not like you *have* to go in."

Penny pursed her lips and squeezed Henny. "Of course I do. It's Saturday."

Right. Penny had worked at the museum every Tuesday through Saturday since she was sixteen. Lately, she'd cut back her hours to part-time, but that was the most she'd ever do. There was no way a little thing like Casper's murder would keep her from cataloging the latest Civil War memorabilia that someone had donated to the old tollhouse-turned-museum.

Paca Springs was a town of about one thousand, named for William Paca, one of the signatories of the Declaration of Independence, whose name I only knew because I lived in a town named after him. I wasn't sure exactly what could be interesting enough about our town to warrant an entire museum, but all East Coast towns had one. It was just what you did. The Civil War alone had ensured there was someone important who had died somewhere nearby.

My sister loved cataloging the numerous effects of the past. She would say museums were the only real way to time travel.

"Besides," said Penny, "it'll give me some time to get my 'little gray cells' working on our problem."

{ 3 }

In Which Grief Hangs Like a Curtain

When we were younger, Penny and I had more in common. In fact, people often asked if we were twins, we were so close in size and shape. No one ever asked that these days.

When I hit puberty I kept growing up, while my sister grew out. We had the same hair color now, of course, and as kids we were both pure blondes. But in the middle of life we were different: my hair going darker toward brown and Penny's going redder toward a beautiful strawberry-blonde. I was always envious of her hair color. I even dyed or highlighted my hair for awhile there to try to imitate hers, but nothing beats natural color.

Which was what I was thinking when I finally found Maya sitting on the bench out by the pond, still holding Casper, her obviously dyed bronze-brown hair creating a mourning curtain as she murmured softly to him.

I approached cautiously, well aware that we all grieve in different ways and uncertain whether Maya was one of the sort that liked to be left alone or liked to have someone to talk to.

I was pleased to see that Tomi and Tuppence had been quietly drawn to her in her time of grief. I absolutely loved my geese. They were extremely friendly and well-mannered. Their yellow-orange beaks looked like snowmen's carrot noses, and their striking, wide orange feet popped out from beneath their white-feathered bodies. The Embden breed of goose was the tallest of geese, known for its swan-like neck and ocean blue eyes. But don't let their good looks fool you: they can protect themselves when they want to. Hissing attack geese were no laughing matter, except for me when I watched them chase off the latest cat that got too crafty for its own good.

Grieving geese, on the other hand, were about as sad as you could get. Their eyes looked so sorrowful, and the way their necks drooped down as they stood beside Maya told me that they were as perceptive of human emotions as any dog. They looked up as I approached, but didn't honk in greeting like usual.

As I neared, I realized Maya wasn't talking, but singing. It was a beautiful song in a foreign language—French or Italian.

She stopped when I sat down next to her.

I didn't say anything, just waited for her to speak while I looked around. The bench she'd chosen was in the holler north of our pond. The pond was not very large, and shallow enough to freeze in the winter so you could ice skate across it. Aunt Connie loved to have her children, grandchildren, and greats out to enjoy it in the snow, though my own grandkids preferred wading and swimming in the pond in the summer.

My son had never shown much interest in it. He was much more fascinated by books. Derrick never had a problem filling the silence, and as a working mother I never would have survived if he hadn't learned to read at the age of six. Now, I know you're thinking every six-year-old learns to read, but not every six-year-old can read *The Audubon Society Field Guide to North American Birds*, much less have it hold their attention.

Derrick's favorite thing to do was to surprise me with little facts he'd learned.

"Did you know the Snow Goose makes a high, nasal sound like 'how-wow?'"

"Did you know the Swainson's Hawk flies in a dihedral or V-angled gliding pattern when soaring on thermal air currents?"

"Did you know the Lawrence's Goldfinch's song incorporates both its own call notes and those of other species?"

After my son moved his family to Colorado Springs and my husband, Sam, passed away, I suppose it was no surprise that geese ended up being my bird of choice. Something had to fill all that irritating silence.

My sister was never interested in marriage. Maybe if she'd found a guy who didn't mind being third wheel to a chicken he'd have had a chance.

When we'd interviewed Maya before she joined the OBS, she'd told us she'd been married and divorced long ago. Said she'd never looked back after realizing making decisions for herself was rather nice. Clearly, she was a woman who liked to be in control.

I wondered if that was the part of Casper's death she was struggling with. The part where she realized she couldn't control life and death. It was probably the most difficult lesson to learn, but we all did, one way or another.

"He was all I had left," Maya whispered to Casper.

His body looked so small in her hands. Maya was roughly a half-foot shorter than me, and I'm over six foot. Her hands were the perfect size for cupping the dead bird.

My heart went out to her. I knew what it was like to lose a pet. I glanced at Tomi and Tuppence. I'd lost a dog or two along the way, and though I hadn't lost a goose yet, I knew Penny had cycled through her share of Hennies, given chickens only live eight years or so.

But I also knew Maya didn't want to hear about our losses right now.

"You've only known us a short while, but trust me when I say we're all here for you."

Maya scoffed and wiped a tear from her cheek. "Not Beatrice."

I hesitated. I knew she was in the midst of grief and it wasn't a good time to contradict her, but I really hated how she'd grasped onto the idea of Beatrice as a murderer. Perhaps it was because I'd been friends with Beatrice since we were ten years old, so I knew how far back her fascination with peacocks and all birds stretched.

"Why do you think Beatrice is the one who did this?" I finally asked.

Maya shook her head. "You wouldn't understand."

"Oh, go on," I urged, nudging her shoulder.

"It doesn't matter," she said with a sigh. "What matters is that Casper will sing no more." She choked on the last word.

"I never heard how you two met."

I know it may sound silly to some, but to the ladies of the OBS, our birds were more than pets, they were family.

I thought I caught the beginning of a smile behind the curtain of bronze hair as Maya began to reminisce.

"I found him at an animal shelter. He was malnourished, but smart as a whip. I took him in and nursed him back to health. He was my...therapy in a way." She wiped another tear. "I'd just had surgery on my throat and discovered it had been unsuccessful. I'd lost my voice, which was like losing a limb for me. It was my life. I'd intended to continue in my career as a professional opera singer until my throat gave out, but that happened a lot sooner than I'd imagined."

"How old were you?"

She sighed heavily. "Forty-three."

Wow. My own son was only forty-one. I couldn't imagine being hit with a life-altering health issue so young.

"But then you found Casper."

"Yes." Again that glimmer of hope. "Then I found Casper. And he gave me my voice back. I couldn't sing, but through him I was able to return to the stage. I trained him to whistle show tunes and soon he was performing four nights a week, and not just as a sideshow for a traveling circus. We were in the big time, performing with symphonies in Seattle, San Francisco, D.C., Philadelphia... We traveled from coast to coast, always on the road. Seeing the nation together."

"Wow, that's impressive."

She smiled for real then, tucking her hair behind her ear, and for a moment she was gazing fondly at the bird in her hand and seeing only his spirit, not his body.

But only for a moment.

Then the light faded. "He sang when I could not," she murmured. "I loved him." Her voice choked. "And now he's dead." She stood in a rush. "I don't care if you believe me or not. Beatrice killed Casper, and I'm going to do something about it."

{ 4 }

In Which We Encounter an Ostentation

Maya was bounding off toward Beatrice's house before I could stop her, moving far more quickly than anyone with such short strides should be capable of doing.

"Wait," I cried, joining her in her walk-run. Tomi and Tuppence followed at my heels, honking excitedly now that we were up and moving. "What are you going to do?"

"I'm going to ask her why she did it, after she'd already taken everything from me, why she had to go and take Casper, too."

"What are you talking about? What has Beatrice done to you?"

But Maya was saving her breath for her sprint as she crossed the grass and wove between the trees to Beatrice Johnson's little cottage. Coming upon it like we did always stirred up images of Hansel and Gretel. The house was a miniature cookie cutter Victorian complete with towers and turrets covered in decorative gingerbread trim. A giant wrap-around porch gave the house a finished look even though it was only a quarter of the size of a typical Victorian mansion. Aunt Connie—the house's original owner—had spared no expense. Then, when Beatrice moved in, she'd given it the final touch, painting it in peacock colors of emerald green, purple, and sapphire blue.

I considered Aunt Connie an honorary member of the OBS since she didn't actually live on our property anymore, though she still came over on her days off to feed the wild quail that gathered in the rushes along the crick, just as she'd done since the day she married my uncle and moved in. In many ways, she was the founding member of the OBS.

When Dad passed in '85 from pancreatic cancer, and we learned the recession had taken its share of his investments, I'd decided to move back in with Penny to help cover expenses. Although it required I retire from my tenure as Victorian Lit professor at Penn State, I'd already been considering it after Sam passed away the year before, also from cancer. Even with Aunt Connie still living in her grandiloquent house with the gingerbread trim, it wasn't enough, and we quickly realized we'd either need to sell parts of our land or take on renters.

As we couldn't bear to part with the land that had been in our family for as long as we could remember, we started with Beatrice, who'd been my friend since our school days. She rented a room in our house and came with peacocks—a bird I thought would be more exotic than they were in real life. They still poop like any other bird, no matter how pretty their feathers.

And their favorite place to poop was from our roof onto our front door step. Talk about a nice way to start your day.

Slings and Sparrows

Needless to say, it soon became apparent Beatrice needed her own place. After a couple months, Aunt Connie decided to move in with her eldest daughter, Jackie, in order to be closer to her café in town, leaving her place for Beatrice.

As we neared the cottage now, Tomi and Tuppence veered off to go honk at the peacocks. Served the peacocks right. Beatrice's peacocks didn't get the memo when she moved; they still insisted on climbing *our* roof every morning to yelp at the sunrise, and warn us throughout the day of intruders like the UPS guy.

Maya marched right up the porch steps, flung open the screen and banged on the hard wood of the front door.

"Beatrice! Beatrice!" she yelled. "I know you're in there!" She paused and seemed to be listening while I caught my breath. "I can hear that blasted machine of yours so I know you're there! Come out here and explain yourself or I'm coming in!"

When still no one appeared to let the irate woman inside, she barreled through the door, with me at her heels in the hopes I could somehow mediate the situation. I could've really used Alice about now—she was the psychiatrist, after all.

Once the front door had slapped shut behind us, I could hear the loud whirring of Beatrice's sewing machine running in her front parlor. The room was covered from floor to ceiling, not with knickknacks or books, but with costumes.

Costumes hung and draped across every surface. Costumes of every size and shape, but mostly in the same brown and green tones. There were petticoats, overskirts, jackets, flouncy shirts, lace shirts, shirt-waists, vests, top hats, bejeweled hats, and goggles, almost all of them sporting a peacock feather in some manner or other.

I first met Beatrice when we were only ten years old. She moved to Paca Springs and we hit it straight off. By Halloween we were knocking on doors side by side, though she was unabashedly ringing doorbells up and down Main Street in a complete Mary Poppins costume, while I was in my homemade "cowgirl" costume, which was simply one of my dad's flannel shirts, my normal jean skirt and boots, and a cowboy hat I'd found in the local thrift store.

Because Beatrice never grew up, she now, at the age of sixty-five, spent her days providing costuming for the local community theater and anyone else who wanted her beautiful, handmade clothing. Between selling her peacock ephemera and her costumes at craft fairs and such, I didn't think she'd ever officially retire.

Maya marched in and plucked a peacock feather and hatpin from a particularly well-decorated hat, carrying it in one hand and Casper in the other as she accosted Beatrice at her workstation.

Beatrice shrieked as Maya thrust the dead bird into view.

"Good heavens, you scared me!" she exclaimed, the room suddenly going silent as her foot left the pedal beneath the sewing machine. She collected herself, her hand going to her silver and black pompadour.

Beatrice was a "method costumer," meaning she changed how she dressed based on her current costuming work. Lately, she was usually found to be sporting a simple white shirt-waist and long skirt, accentuated by an Edwardian corseted form and petticoats, complete with a pompadour hairstyle. She even wore a chatelaine upon her belt, from which hung the accoutrements of the seamstress, including a miniature pair of scissors, a pincushion, and a tiny silver holder for needles.

It seemed pretty clear why Beatrice had a penchant for ostentations of peacocks.

And yes, that's what a group of peacocks is called: an ostentation. I couldn't make this stuff up.

"Why did you do it, Beatrice?" Maya asked, getting straight to the point.

Beatrice raised a pencil-lined eyebrow, glanced at me and back to Maya, confusion clearly etched across her burnt-umber face. "I don't know what you're talking about. Perhaps you best start at the beginning and explain why you're waving a dead bird in my face."

Maya's face heated to boiling—I could feel it from across the room. "This is Casper. You killed him."

Beatrice shot up out of her chair, removing the thick glasses she only wore when she was sewing, her lips parted in a look of utter shock. "How could you possibly accuse me of such a terrible thing?"

"Ha! You don't deny it!"

"Of course I deny it. I did no such thing! Good heavens— Why? Why would you think that I'd hurt your dear little bird?"

"Because we found him with one of these," Maya held forth the hatpin and attached feather next to the cockatiel, "through his chest this morning."

{ 5 }

In Which We Unfurl a Feather or Two

Beatrice's brown eyes widened and her jaw dropped in a very unladylike manner.

"I'm afraid it's true, Beatrice," I put in, hoping I could smooth over the tension in the room and give Beatrice a chance to explain herself, if she needed to. "Penny and I saw it." I pulled out the actual pin that had done the dirty deed. "Do you recognize this?"

Beatrice slowly drew her eyes away from Casper and looked at what I held.

"Th-that's one of mine," she stuttered, her face in complete disbelief. She reached out and took the pin. "But that doesn't amount to a hill o' beans. Anyone might've taken it." She waved her arms about her in a circle at the mess of costumes. "I'm working on the costumes for the *Wizard of Oz* community theater production. They're doing it in a steampunk style and I've been at sixes and sevens for the past week putting the finishing touches on." She whipped around, her chatelaine clinking as she leaned over her workspace and grabbed a bowl full of more hatpins just like the one I'd handed to her. "You see. These li'l babies are all over the place right now."

I noticed that next to that small bowl had been two more with medium and small pins, but neither looked like the ones we thought had come from Casper's feet.

"You're the only one on the acreage who has them, though," Maya pointed out, forcefully pointing the pin in her hand at Beatrice like she was ready to shish-kabob the woman.

"I swear I was up all night working on costumes. Been up all night every night getting ready for tech week. The director wants a full dress rehearsal starting Monday, and it's already Saturday!"

"Do you have proof?" Maya asked.

"Girl, hold your horses." Beatrice set down the bowl of pins and looked around, as though searching for something. "Now where did I put those ruby..."

Maya gave a short intake of breath and then I heard her blow out slowly, like she was trying desperately to calm down. The length of time it took for Beatrice to find what she wanted amongst all the costumes, however, soon led to Maya's teeth grinding in frustration.

"I know I had them here a minute ago...," Beatrice muttered, throwing up yet another pair of green shoes, but no ruby slippers.

"Ah!" she breathed, before pouncing on a particularly elaborate costume covered in green sequins, hidden beneath a pile of skirts on the couch. "This'll have to do. I was working on this last night. I swear this jacket was only a bit of jade fabric when I started after supper and now just look at it!"

She held it out and it shimmered in the light of the sun streaming through the window.

"How do we know you're telling the truth?" Maya asked with a frown.

"How do you know she's not?" I countered.

"You can ask Billy Bacon, if you'd like," Beatrice said.

"Billy Bacon?" I asked. Was there really a man going through life with such a moniker?

"Sure thing," said Beatrice with a nod and a big grin. "William T. Bacon, the most gorgeous man you've ever seen. This is his costume. He's playing the Wizard in the show, you know, even though he's played the biggest houses all up and down the coast. Even tried his hand on Broadway for a spell, till he realized he could do more with his talents in the wilds of the local theaters."

I bit back a snort. Sounded to me like he'd failed and settled, but I could see the sparkles in Beatrice's eyes and knew she wouldn't take kindly to my disbelief.

"He was kind enough to give me his measurements last night at supper." Beatrice giggled like a schoolgirl and gave a wink in my direction.

"Ugh!" Maya threw up the hand with the pin in it and slammed it down beside Beatrice's sewing machine, somehow managing not to stick herself. Then she spun on her heel and marched out the door, turning only to announce fiercely, "You are *not* invited to the funeral."

"Good heavens," Beatrice muttered again once we were alone.

Slings and Sparrows

"You wouldn't happen to have any idea why Maya is convinced you'd murder her bird, would you?"

"Absolutely not," declared Beatrice, sitting with great distinction back on her sewing chair. "I had no idea she disliked me so."

"She's obviously upset with you over something. Have you two fought recently?"

"I honestly have no idea what she might have against me."

I had a couple guesses, and they included any man Beatrice had flirted with since Maya's arrival. Beatrice had a tendency to flirt with anything male and standing on two legs. She was worse than the peacocks sometimes, who would display for even the guinea hens when they wandered by. No matter what era she was dressed in, she'd always been in love with flirtatious modus operandi, from the secret fan language (touching the handle to your lips meant "kiss me") to the meaning behind stamp placement on a letter (placed upside down in the left upper corner meant "I love you"). It all seemed silly to me since it required that the male of the species understand what the flirtatious signals meant, but I suppose, like so many birds, we all knew what the unfurling of a peacock's feathers signified.

"Bless her heart," murmured Beatrice with a shake of her head. Her time living in North Carolina still showed through in some of her phrases, even though she'd spent most of her life in PA and we'd tried our hardest to train it out of her—like calling the state "Pee-Ay" and not "Pennsylvania."

She replaced her sewing glasses upon her nose. "Well, I'm afraid I must get back to work. These costumes won't sew themselves. Let me know if there's anything I can do to help. Anything at all."

"Has anyone come by recently to look at your costumes?" I asked.

"No one." Beatrice paused, considering something. "Course, when my machine gets going, as you saw, I can't really hear nothing going on around me. I suppose it's possible anyone might've helped themselves to a pin without my ever even noticing."

That was encouraging. "Including Mr. Bacon? How often have you seen him this week?"

Beatrice had the courtesy to blush. "At supper last night he told me he can't see me anymore so close to opening night. Says I'd only distract him from his performance." She giggled again and I was certain if she'd had a fan she'd have fluttered it before her face coquettishly. "We won't be getting together again till after closing, other than rehearsals. He's a true professional."

I nodded, but she hadn't exactly answered my question.

"You might talk to Sable," Beatrice said, twisting in her seat and preparing her fabric for more stitching. "Piercing birds through their chests sounds like something from an Edgar Allan Poe poem. Perhaps she was simply reenacting a Poe story and got carried away?"

{ 6 }

In Which We Learn Goths Have a Sense of Humor

It was a good thing it was Saturday, or I knew I wouldn't have caught Sable at home. During the week, she worked at the Penn State Extensions in Mcconnellsburg, Bedford, and Chambersburg, which were all about a thirty to forty-five minute drive from Paca Springs. She rotated her time working in the agricultural centers at each one. Something to do with soil samples and greenhouses and urban gardening, that sort of thing. Sable Amsel was one of those unsung geniuses who will be indispensable in the future when technology fails us and we finally realize we should've stuck to farming and living off the land all along.

I found Sable as usual in her garden, dressed in her standard attire of black boots, black jeans, and a black t-shirt. Unlike most of our brood who still had some of her original hair color, and her face was as smooth as a baby's bottom, brown like chai tea thanks to her half-Filipino heritage. She'd let her hair go naturally, and it did so in a beautiful manner that manifested in streams of silver through her straight jet-black hair. She normally wore it pulled back in a single braid, which produced an extremely pleasing woven effect.

She moved onto our land two years after Beatrice, but her arrival was more silent and stealthy, as she only came with one bird, a raven named Hugin. Apparently, Hugin was one of the Norse god Odin's ravens, whose name meant "thought." It was just like Sable to have a raven named Thought.

Sable and Penny and I got along very well, so long as we stuck to our one common topic of conversation: literature. As soon as someone made the mistake of asking Sable about a flower or plant, however, I felt my eyes glaze over as I switched to simply nodding my head and smiling, as I hadn't the foggiest notion what a *Bellis perennis* was or what the benefits of the *Lumbricina* were (a daisy and an earthworm if you're wondering—don't fall for that whole "you can't teach an old dog new tricks" routine).

Thus, I approached with hesitation when I found Sable on her hands and knees taking soil samples. I hoped we could make this quick.

"Hello!" I called out, and she greeted me in kind. Her smile was as friendly as a daffodil, if daffodils wore black. "I need your help with something," I began.

"Shoot," Sable replied with a nod, standing and brushing dirt off her knees.

"I was wondering what you were up to last night."

"Let's see…last night I stayed up late reading *Dracula* and then fell asleep after a full cup of blood. B Positive, if you're wondering. Figured I could use a little silver lining on these dreary days." She smiled at the clouds as they scuttled across the sky.

I gave her a polite laugh, acknowledging her joke with a shake of my head. "Come on, be serious," I said. "I know for a fact you prefer Shelley over Stoker any day. But admit it: you were reading *Northanger Abbey* again."

Sable made a face. She was *not* a Jane Austen fan. "Guilty," Sable said, brushing a stray hair from her cheek with the back of her gloved hand. "Seriously, though, why are you asking?"

I hesitated. I'd hoped to get her answer without revealing my hand, but I leaned over her garden fence and told her what we'd found that morning.

She shook her head sadly at the news. "I'm so sorry to hear that. I know if anything happened to Hugin I'd be devastated. Let me know what I can do to help."

"Would you mind telling me what you did last night? For real this time?"

Sable smiled. "I don't mind. I went to bed and read a book, like I said."

"What book?"

"*The Prestige.*"

"Haven't heard of it."

"It's relatively new. Won the World Fantasy Award for Best Novel last year. Hold on a sec and I'll get it for you. I stayed up till two in the morning finishing it. I think you'd really like it: it's epistolary, most of it takes place in Victorian England, and it has a fabulous twist at the end that I did *not* see coming."

I stood up and followed Sable inside. She lived in a tiny house, which in comparison to Beatrice's felt like the size of a quail egg. Its compact nature was perfect for Sable, who was a good foot shorter than me and was really only at home on the weekends. Sable swore compact living was the future, and she might have been on to something given how much she saved each month on utilities.

We were greeted by Hugin, who ruffled his feathers as though he'd just woken from a nap. He flew down from his perch to land on the back of the couch.

"Hello! How are you?" he croaked.

"I'm fine. Thank you for asking," I replied.

"Nice to see you, nice to see you."

"You, too." I nodded to Hugin. "Such a polite bird," I said to Sable.

Sable set down her test tubes, trowel, and gloves and kicked off her boots before climbing into her lofted bed to grab the book. Sable was one of those irritating women who was still incredibly fit even at sixty-two, and would probably remain so well into her eighties.

"You're only as old as you think you are," Beatrice liked to say whenever I remarked on things like that.

"Then I must be as old as a steam train, 'cause I think I'm running out of track," I'd say.

I knew one thing for sure: age was relative. Aunt Connie could still out-maneuver me and she was in her mid-eighties.

"Here you go," Sable said, handing me the paperback. It looked almost new, but the spine told of at least one read, so I supposed that worked for me as confirmation of Sable's alibi. "Guess you'll have to read it pretty fast so you can ask me questions about it to confirm my story," she said, reading my mind.

I smiled. "I wouldn't know anything about that; it's Penny who's the real mystery buff."

"So you keep telling me, yet you're the one who waxes eloquent on the history of the genre."

"Can I help it the Golden Age was inspired by Victorian lit?"

"You wouldn't happen to know anyone who teaches that subject, would you?" Sable asked sarcastically, reminding me perhaps I needed to bring my enthusiasm down a notch. "Where is Penny anyway?"

"She's working at the museum as usual."

"She didn't take a grief day?"

"If it had been Henny, she would've, but neither of us really know Maya or Casper all that well yet. They've only been here a few weeks."

"It's been over two months now, hasn't it?" Sable asked, giving Hugin a pet before pulling her boots back on.

"Has it really?" I whistled. "Wow. Time does fly."

"Time does fly, time does fly," Hugin repeated.

"That's a good one for you to know," I said.

I watched Sable grab her things off the counter again as a thought occurred to me. "You wouldn't happen to know why Maya might be angry at Beatrice, would you? Beatrice swears she has no idea why Maya is convinced she's the one who killed her bird—other than the fact that it was one of her hatpins, but like she said, anyone might have grabbed one of those."

It seemed to me that Sable hesitated, but she might've just been waiting for Hugin to decide whether he'd be joining us outside or not. The raven nodded once and flew out ahead of us as soon as the door opened, soaring up into the sky.

"No." She held her hand up to shade her eyes as the sun poked through the clouds and hit us on our way out. "I did overhear Maya and Aunt Connie arguing the other day, though."

Everyone called our Aunt Connie "Aunt Connie" or "Auntie." Probably had something to do with the fact that with four married daughters, sixteen grandchildren, and four great-grandchildren, almost everyone in town was related to her in some degree.

What could anyone have against Aunt Connie?

"I'm not sure what it was about," Sable said with a shrug. She walked back through her gate and closed it. "You know, what really seems odd to me is the fact that those smaller pins, along with the holes you found in the dowel rod, imply that Casper's feet were pinned to his perch. Who would do something like that? But more importantly, *how* would someone do that?"

"I know what you mean," I said. "I don't know of a single bird who'd sit still long enough to have its feet pinned down."

"What if he was pinned down so he couldn't fly away from the hatpin coming toward him?"

"That's what I wondered. Any bird worth its salt should be able to avoid a flying hatpin."

"He must've been drugged to get him pinned down," Sable said, "but if the person had the drugs, why not just kill him that way?"

"And why do something so pointless? It's clearly a slight against Maya, but who doesn't like her?"

"Do you know anything about her past that might help?"

I shook my head. "I need to do some more digging." I waved toward the trowel and other implements in Sable's hands. "Clearly you do, too, so I'll leave you to it."

And with that, I left Sable with her knees in the dirt, and began to follow my nose toward Aunt Connie's café and the sweet smell of the best croissants this side of the Mason-Dixon.

{ 7 }

In Which I Eat Far Too Much Food

The Quaint Quail was only about a mile and a half from where Sable's house sat on our sixty-seven acres. Aunt Connie had been running it for as long as I could remember, though it had changed some over the years. In its earliest form, it was a soda fountain, then it went through a phase as a sub shop, followed by a very short-lived attempt at being a game store—Aunt Connie's family was crazy about family game night—until finally landing on the money maker: a literary tea shop.

My cousin, Jacqueline, or "Jackie," Aunt Connie's eldest, was the one who came up with the idea, so The Quaint Quail was as much her baby as Aunt Connie's.

It was the epitome of the small-town, family-run establishment. Jackie's husband, James, was an accountant in Paca Springs, and helped out at the café when he was needed, which was usually to wash dishes. Jackie's eldest daughter, Juliette, was being primed to take over the business someday, once her children were old enough.

"Feels like that'll never happen," she'd said to me before.

"I know you hear this a lot, but I promise, someday you'll miss the crazy," I told her.

It was true. Whenever my son came to visit and brought his three kids, I soaked up the crazy, and then, admittedly with some great pleasure, sent them home again.

As the shop bell rang upon my entrance, I was welcomed with a hearty hug from Jackie, who was old enough herself to be a member of the OBS. She always said she was just fine for now, so long as her husband was living, which I appreciated, as I've tried to keep the OBS a strictly females-only establishment.

I followed the sound of jazz music into the kitchen, where I found Aunt Connie with a bowl of muffin batter in one hand and a spoon in the other, held to her lips like a microphone as she offered her best Billie Holiday impression.

The first thing you noticed about Aunt Connie was her hair. She had irresistible soft, cloud-white curls that piled high on top of her pale head, giving her some much-needed extra height. One curl in particular always refused to stay put and usually stuck straight up and out like a quail's top-feather, which was probably where she got the name for her establishment. Like Penny, she was short and round and a little firecracker of energy. Life was never dull with Aunt Connie around.

The second thing you noticed about Aunt Connie was that she never stopped moving. And I mean that literally. The day Aunt Connie sat down was the day Jesus returned, and she'd be the first to tell you that. Nowadays they'd probably say she had that ADHD or ADD thing, but since she never stood still long enough to even think about getting diagnosed, we just said she was Aunt Connie. And Aunt Connie never stopped for more than a second without having to do "just one more thing."

Aunt Connie opened her eyes after her jazz solo and threw the spoon into the bowl and onto the counter in one fluid motion.

"Goose!" she cried. "You look hungry. Let me get you something to eat."

Penny and I probably took for granted the fact that Aunt Connie always insisted on pampering us with free food whenever we were in the vicinity of her café. In fact, with all the family discounts she offered, and with a quarter of the town considered "family," whether by blood or not, it was a wonder she managed to stay in business.

It was no use telling her I had no appetite, as she'd whip up a plate full of a little bit of everything for me no matter what I said, and the truth of the matter was, I was getting a mite hungry.

What felt like an hour later, my belly gurgled happily, filled to the brim with some Much Ado About Muffins, Brothers Carrot-mazov, Fellowship of the Onion Rings, War and Peach Pie, and freshly brewed Don Quixotea to wash it all down.

I realized it would be yet another hour before I could walk home again in this condition, so I might as well take my time and scoop up Penny on the way back, as the museum was just down the road and she'd be off soon. There was only one main street in Paca Springs, which ran directly down the middle of the thin mile-and-a-half strip known as Maryland's narrow waist.

That's right: Paca Springs was technically in Maryland, though our land, which was just a short walk away, was in PA. West Virginia was a few blocks to the west, too, making us ideally placed for lots of local discussion as to whether one considered oneself a Pennsylvanian, West Virginian, or a Marylander.

I was a world traveler myself, breaking all the rules, though if I had to choose, I'd probably associate with Pennsylvanians the most.

Aunt Connie broke all the rules herself, too, as she danced beside my table asking again if I was sure I wouldn't have anymore.

"I couldn't fit another—," I stopped myself, because if I named anything she'd only respond by saying that particular thing "filled in the cracks."

Instead, I tried to distract her with questioning. "How do you ever find the time to make all this food, Auntie? I can hardly find the time to toast one of those microwave toaster pastries. I usually just eat them straight out of the box."

I knew immediately I might have accidentally offended her. Packaged food made Aunt Connie cringe deep inside because why would anyone spend money on terrible products when they could just whip up a batch of New Orleans-style beignets? But not all of us were blessed with Aunt Connie's talents.

"I don't mind it. In my opinion it's time well-spent. Every night, Jackie and I prep the dough for the next day, so that we can begin first thing in the morning, which means every night I get some special time with my daughter I might not have gotten otherwise. Neither of us is getting any younger, and the world gets busier and quicker every day. We need to slow down once in a while and let the dough rise, you know what I'm saying?" Auntie said in her prolific wisdom.

"You were here with Jackie last night?"

"Sure shootin'. We walked home together admiring the moon."

I didn't doubt it. Aunt Connie never lied.

"I wondered if you might have seen something last night on your walk home. Did you hear what happened to Maya's cockatiel?"

I filled her in as she continued to bounce from counter to counter whipping up batches of goodness—croissants, macarons, sugar cookies, and other inspirations from her life of travel—for the front of house.

"How dreadful," she said, her hand to her heart, as I finished. She bowed her head and I wondered if she was sending up a prayer for the bird right then and there, being a Baptist and all. "Maya and I were just talking the other day about Casper."

"Oh?"

"I was trying again to get Maya to teach that bird to whistle jazz, but she said he only did show tunes."

I almost laughed. Was this the argument Sable had overheard? "Did you guys fight?"

"Fight? Nah!" Auntie waved her hand. "We just talked." She swayed to a new song that was playing, her quail curl bobbing in time. "And danced."

"Maya danced with you?"

"Well," Auntie winked, "she tried."

{ 8 }

In Which We Ask Questions Without Answers

Penny sat in front of her computer in the back room of the museum, but her fingers were busy running over and through Henny's soft feathers, nowhere near the keyboard, as she stared at the blank screen.

"Penny?" I asked as softly as I could, but I still made her jump a little at my voice. She must've squeezed Henny a bit for she clucked suddenly like a bagpipe.

"Good gracious, Goose," she said. "What are you doing here?"

"I came to walk you home."

Penny smiled. It's funny: to me, she hadn't aged a day. When I looked at her, I could still see the little girl in twin blonde braids who'd spend every moment she could curled up against my shoulder while I read to her. Our favorite place in the world was nestled with a good book. We could be in a tree, by a stream, on a bench, on a couch, or in the library, but we were always found with a book.

"How was your day?" Penny asked, pulling on a light sweater and following me out the door. She never carried a purse anywhere, just a chicken.

"Good. You?"

Penny shrugged. "I've been very distracted. I don't think I got a thing done." Her brow creased. "I honestly have a difficult time remembering what I did all day."

I bit my tongue from saying, "At least it's only mindless data entry." Penny might have felt defensive of that description of her work, though it was true. The computer was a new but necessary addition to the tiny museum. It was honestly like something out of *The Twilight Zone* to me and Penny, and I couldn't help but compare ourselves to the turn of the last century, when the advances in technology completely changed the world in which the Victorians and Gilded Age Americans were living.

Given it was clear the new technology wasn't going anywhere anytime soon, it was now Penny's job to start transferring the cabinets of physical card data cataloging every item in the museum, both on display and in storage, into the computer. It would make searching for items for researchers so much easier, but the mindlessness of simply copying everything off a tiny handwritten card into a computer was something only someone like Penny, with her extreme attention to detail, would find any sort of enjoyable.

"Have you been using your 'little gray cells'?" I asked instead.

She smiled. "I suppose I have, though they haven't gotten me anywhere yet."

"We've both had a lot to process today. It's been far from ordinary."

"It certainly has," Penny said with a deep breath and a shake of her head. "Have you spoken with Maya?"

"Yeah." I told her about our talk on the bench, our run-in with Beatrice, my follow-up with Sable, and my afternoon lunch at Aunt Connie's.

"My goodness, you've had a full day," Penny said once I'd finished. "All I've done is come up with a list of questions."

"What are they?"

She numbered them off on the hand clutching Henny as she answered. "Why were Casper's feet pinned to his perch? How did the hatpin fly through the bars of his cage and pierce him so perfectly? Why would someone want to hurt Maya that way?"

"Good questions." I nodded. "I didn't find answers to any of them this morning."

"Then I suppose our day is not yet finished."

We turned off the sidewalk and followed the deer path that would take us north, across the border, and back into PA and our little parcel of land. I said "little" but I was well aware that sixty-seven acres was a goodly portion compared to most places on the East Coast. Heck, when Sam and I lived in the city we considered a yard of *any* size a bonus.

Penny and I had been very lucky to inherit the home we'd grown up in along with the land we'd rambled over and explored all of our childhood, even though it took a bit of creative thinking to keep the place. What with taxes here and taxes there, it was difficult to understand how a body could keep hold of land that had come relatively cheap to our grandfather and practically free to our father. I supposed they'd still paid a cost working the land—for a time as a dairy farm, and later as a sheep farm—just perhaps not a financial one.

Penny and I had grown up walking that mile and a half between the property and town. We knew it like the back of our hand, and in some ways better, since our hands had been getting new liver spots lately.

Walking was really my only form of exercise these days, which explained why I may not be the trimmest woman over six feet tall. And even then, some days we took the four-wheeler into town instead of walking. There was a great path that many people used for walking and running and biking that ran along the edge of our property into town. We used to bike it everyday as kids, into town to get milk, always two gallons at a time, as we'd have to ride back with milk jugs balanced on the handlebars. The story of Penny building her first chicken-seat onto her bike for Henny is a funny one, but I'll save it for later. Right now, we had business to attend to.

Our land was marked by a fence, on which we'd set a couple Private Property and No Hunting signs. Everyone in town knew he or she could find a plethora of birds on our property. We'd talked about filing for an official permit to turn our land into a government-protected animal reserve, but it was a bureaucratic nightmare around here getting anything like that done because of the way three state borders bumped up against one another.

As we crossed the fence, Penny voiced aloud a new thought, somewhat connected to my own train of thinking.

"You know, *anyone* could have come onto our property and killed Casper."

"I was thinking a similar thing," I said. "But we've never had any problems before. I could see someone sneaking over to have a crack at a duck for an easy dinner, possibly even a guinea fowl if they're feeling exotic, but to kill a cockatiel? And in such a crazy way. They even left the body behind. It just makes no sense."

"Murder never does," Penny said solemnly.

"I mean, literally anyone might have come into our house to kill Casper. It's not like we lock our doors at night." We never had. That's how safe the area felt.

"Perhaps we'd better start doing that tonight," said Penny softly, and I realized I'd just inadvertently given her something new to fear. It was my goal in life to avoid doing exactly that.

Penny's anxiety was usually not linked to actual problems. She suffered more from just constant worry about generalities. What if we ran out of food? (We never would as we'd stockpiled enough to hold us over through a third World War.) What if we ran out of water? (See stockpile.) What if the government raised taxes so high we lost our land and had to live on the streets? (Honestly, even I sometimes worried about this one, though I knew we would be taken in by family in town.) But it had never occurred to Penny to be anxious about burglars or murderers. She'd been born and raised and never left Paca Springs, so everyone knew her and she knew everyone. So there was nothing to fear.

Certainly, as our little OBS group could attest, there were new people passing through all the time, and some of them stuck around. But somehow this had never worried her, probably because a stranger in Paca Springs stuck out like a sore thumb, and the entire town would know the person's name, address, date of birth, and favorite flavor of ice cream before they'd stopped to ask for directions.

"We need to talk to Maya," I said, trying to distract Penny's whirling thoughts that I could already see were coming out through her fingers and into Henny. "This has nothing to do with us."

"Except that she's in our house."

"Yes, but there's something she's not telling us. Some reason someone has it out for her. Something from her past. This is all about her and not about us."

Penny nodded but didn't seem to agree.

Thankfully, at that moment, Tomi and Tuppence waddled up to us, honking and gabbling excitedly.

"Well, hello, there. Nice of you to join us," I said.

I listened to them telling me all about their day as I nodded.

"Wow, sounds like you two had quite the adventure," I said. By the way, I think it's crazy that some people *don't* talk to animals.

"Honk," said Tomi.

"Honk, honk," said Tuppence.

"Well, how about that? Tuppence says, 'It is a great advantage to be intelligent and not to look it,'" I quoted.

I got a smile out of Penny for that one. "Don't put yourself down, Tuppence. I think you're gorgeous," said Penny. Henny gave a soft cluck at her side. "You, too, Henny."

"She's just quoting her namesake, though in this case the quote in *Partners in Crime* is actually Christie quoting *another* detective, M. Hanaud from A. E. W. Mason's story *At the Villa Rose*."

"Thank you, professor." Penny smiled. "And Tomi? What did she have to say?"

"She said, 'Two minds are always better than one, especially when solving a tricky crime.'"

"Very true. Also from Christie?"

"Of course."

Tomi and Tuppence continued honking.

"They also say we need to go talk to Alice. She may have some thoughts on the psychological angles of the whole Maya debacle."

I thanked the geese and we turned toward the pond, circling to the south side. Tomi and Tuppence followed us until they realized where we were headed, and then apparently decided they'd rather not deal with those particular birds today.

As the honks of Tomi and Tuppence faded into the background, a new sound began to fill the air as we neared Alice Ledford's home.

"Thank God she picked the farthest spot from our house," I murmured, as the ratcheting sound of a crazed guinea fowl reached our ears.

{ 9 }

In Which We Attempt to Find a Clean Seat

Alice Ledford was almost as crazy as her birds. One guinea fowl in particular seemed to always be suffering from an existential crisis, forever crying out, "The sky is falling! The sky is falling!" which should've been Henny's line.

Her house looked perfectly normal on the outside: a small manufactured home that had been expanded and given more permanence in the seven years Alice had been on OBS land. But on the inside? Well, let's just say her home was the perfect example of the type of people who generally went to people like Alice.

Unfortunately, as we approached, the sun was covered by an impending accumulation of clouds, causing a chill to descend rapidly. Which meant when Alice came to the door, she beckoned us inside and out of the weather.

The sweet smell of mothballs greeted our noses and the thick sound of silence caused by being in such a closed-in space made me wonder at how Penny ever managed to visit without feeling claustrophobic.

Hoarders ain't got nothing on Alice.

Stacks of books, magazines, and paraphernalia crowded the main room as we entered. Shelves covered in esoteric devices from around the world featuring planets, stars, and the cosmos at large all seemed to be looking at me from within their dusty confines. A model of the solar system stood next to a wooden chess set which was next to three geodes displaying their sparkling crystalized innards in blue, green, and purple. There was no organization to it all that I could see. It was like whenever she acquired something new she just added it to a shelf or pile somewhere. I wondered how she ever found anything.

Even though her square footage was technically more than Sable's, I found myself longing for the clean, organized openness of my friend's small home.

Alice kindly moved a couple stacks of collected magazines off of a dusty, tattered loveseat, inviting us to sit down while she set the stacks on the floor, where they promptly did an admirable impression of the Leaning Tower of Pisa.

Alice's dyed purple-red hair was pulled back in a bun, as usual, though I had seen it down once and was amazed to see it reached the middle of her back. Penny and I waved away her offer of something to drink, then waited for her to take her own seat.

Before we could say anything, a continuous noise like a squeaky gate grew louder outside as the crazed guinea fowl decided to converge on the nearby window.

"Shut up, Freud!" Alice yelled out the open window. Of course, the bird didn't stop but continued to make his *ach, ach* sound. She shook her head and turned to find a seat, though she forgot to close the window as she did so.

Thankfully, Freud seemed to have gotten the attention he wanted from his mistress, as his call lightened in ferocity as he continued to move away from the house.

"So, what can I do for you ladies?" Alice's slow, deep voice always surprised me.

"We're here about Maya's bird," I began. "Have you heard the news?"

Alice's mouth turned downward. "Yes, I'm afraid I have. Maya came here herself to ask who I would suspect, and seemed quite put out that I didn't agree with her theory that it was Beatrice."

"May I ask why you *don't* think it was her?" Penny asked softly.

Alice pushed up her large, round glasses with an olive-brown hand, but they simply sank down to rest on her cheeks again. "It seems clear to me that Beatrice does not have the psychology for the type of person who would kill a bird. Much less in such an abhorrent manner. Maya is obviously upset with Beatrice over something else completely. They've been at odds for quite some time."

"You've noticed tension between them?" I asked.

"Ha," Alice laughed, "that's putting it mildly. Maya and Beatrice have hated each other almost from the first moment they met."

I raised my eyebrows. "Really? I hadn't noticed."

Alice turned her heavy-lidded gaze upon me, which made me nervous, like her psychologist background was about to jump out and bite me. "I'm not surprised. You generally remain unaware of the affairs of those outside your circle."

"You're saying Beatrice might have been flirting with Maya's ex-husband?"

Alice touched her glasses again. "I did not mean an actual affair. I meant that unless an event occurs that involves Penny, you tend not to notice."

Ouch. That seemed a bit harsh.

"That seems a bit harsh," Penny said, and I gave her a grateful smile.

"Do *you* know why Beatrice and Maya are angry at each other?" I asked, pressing forward with the matter at hand.

"I do not. But given it is Beatrice, I have no doubt it involves a man. As it's quite difficult to keep track of the current man in her life, I suppose it might be easier to ask Maya whom she's been seeing instead."

She had a point. However, I was one up on Alice. I knew who Beatrice was seeing at the moment, and Maya had blasted Beatrice right after hearing about how he "shared his measurements" with her.

"What about you? Have you anything against Maya at the moment?" Penny asked, her grip firm on Henny.

Alice brushed her nose. "Absolutely not."

"Do you have an alibi for last night?"

"An alibi? This is not a murder mystery."

"Sure it is. A bird has been murdered," I said.

Alice sniffed lightly and gave a derogatory smile, but she obliged. "No, I don't have an *alibi*. And I don't need one. I know where I was and I know I didn't do it and that's all that matters." Alice stood. "If that's all, I need to wash my hair."

Wow. No one had used the old "washing my hair" excuse since *Bye, Bye Birdie*.

"Thank you for your time," Penny said as she stood. But I wasn't finished.

"Alice," I said, leaning forward intently, my hands clasped, "we need your help."

Alice *loved* to be viewed as a wise woman with all the answers. If she'd lived in the Gilded Age, she'd have made a very handsome living as a spiritualist or fortune teller, using her gift of psychiatry and ability to read people as a way of telling people the Truth.

Alice pushed her glasses up again. "I don't see how I can be of any help."

"Only you can create a psychological profile of the type of person who'd do such a terrible thing to one of our birds," Penny said, clearly realizing the same thing I had about the best way to get Alice to share. "Only you can bring justice to Maya's aching heart. She trusts you."

Alice sniffed. Then she smiled. "You're right."

The moment was interrupted by another rendition of "Squeaky Hinges" by Freud, but I knew I'd gotten through to Alice. Penny did, too, as she sank back down onto the loveseat, a small puff of dust rising and settling again to either side.

"So, what are your thoughts in regards to this case?" I asked, surrendering the floor to Alice.

Alice's shoulders straightened. In my mind's eye she curved one hand about a crystal ball and beckoned the glow within to life while she touched her hand to her forehead.

"Maya is suffering greatly after this heinous act."

Uh, duh, I wanted to say.

"She could barely come to grips with the reality of it when she was with me. All she could do was talk about how Casper had saved her career when she'd given up hope. How he'd given his wings when hers had been clipped. It was quite sad to hear her speak of such things. Sadder still to see her warring between grief and her true feelings."

"True feelings?" I repeated.

"Yes." Alice pushed her glasses up once more. "She clearly was jealous of her bird."

I almost laughed out loud. "What?"

"Maya was jealous of Casper's time in the spotlight. She longed to be the one receiving acclaim."

"I can understand that," Penny murmured beside me and I turned to her. She shrugged. "Imagine having aspirations to be the best singer in the world, only to have your place taken by a whistling cockatiel."

"Just like Julie Andrews," said a voice outside the window.

I leapt from my seat, imagining Freud had somehow learned to speak. But as the voice was rather brusque and lacked that ratcheting quality, I soon realized to whom it belonged.

"Hello, Ruth."

{ 10 }

In Which Julie Andrews is Mentioned Again

"Pardon my interrupting," Ruth Collingwood said from the open window, the high ground outside providing her with the ability to lean against the outer sill as though she'd just popped by for tea. "I was just out for a brisk walk and thought I'd stop in, but I see you have company."

"Walk" being the operative word, seeing as she was more like a brooding duck when she got off her nest and waddled awkwardly for a quick meal and a bath before hobbling back.

Alice beckoned for Ruth to come join us, and she did, hobbling into the small living room. Ruth had an old war wound—don't worry, I'm sure it will come up in conversation at some point—that meant she walked with a cane.

Today she was wearing a brown tweed ensemble that looked remarkably like a hunting costume worn at the turn of the century. Her close-cropped gray hair was mostly hidden beneath a matching hat, which she removed upon entrance, running her fingers through her bob to fluff it.

"I couldn't help but overhear you discussing Maya's mixed feelings toward her beloved stage partner. It brings to mind the scene in Mary Poppins where Julie Andrews must share the spotlight with a whistling animatronic robin."

"Wasn't it actually Julie Andrews doing the whistling in that scene?" I asked.

"Yes, I believe I read that somewhere. The woman could do anything. Then she lost her voice. Bloody throat nodules."

Of course, in Ruth's case, she meant "bloody" as a British curse word, being an avid Anglophile. The first time I heard her use it, I misunderstood her after traipsing through her living room wearing muck boots I'd forgotten to remove at the door. "They're muddy, not bloody," I said, to which she immediately set me straight.

She even attempted a slight British accent when she spoke, as though her brief visits overseas to see her daughter—who was stationed there with the Air Force—would cause such an affectation. Now, I loved British lit as much as the next person, but picking up an accent by reading was a bit much. Still, I could always rely on Ruth for an excellent discussion regarding the latest British crime drama airing on PBS's Mystery!

"I'm pretty sure I read somewhere that Julie Andrews didn't actually have throat nodules," Alice said tentatively. One always had to be tentative when correcting Ruth.

"What?" Ruth flared. Sure enough, her grip on her cane tightened.

"Yes, it was something else, but the point is, the surgeons apparently went in and botched it up. I hope she sues them."

"Really?" Penny asked.

Alice nodded. "I think in Maya's case, however, it really was throat nodules that caused her to quit singing."

"Well," said Ruth, slightly mollified that at least someone had throat nodules, "I suppose I'll have to ask her sometime."

"Not today, though," I put in. "She won't be in the mood to discuss anything, much less what caused her to share the limelight with Casper in the first place."

"And why would that be?" Ruth asked, her gray eyebrows raised.

"He was skewered this morning," I said bluntly, tired of repeating myself. Thankfully, it was Penny who jumped in and told Ruth what had happened, and much nicer than I would have.

Ruth leaned on her cane and shook her head, clucking her tongue at the news. "I'm gutted. Absolutely gutted. And here I was busy watching *Poirot* last night, completely unaware of the murderous situation occurring not a hundred yards from my own front door."

"They started a new series?" Penny asked excitedly.

"No, it was a rerun."

"Which one?"

"Oh, I can never remember the name of the novel it's based on, but it's the one with the dog who witnesses the murder and is blamed for it since the woman trips on his ball and falls down the stairs."

"*Dumb Witness*," Penny said promptly. "I do so hope the series is picked up again. I had hoped they'd make it through all of the Poirot novels, but they've only done a handful of full-length episodes and a bunch of the short stories."

"Is *Dumb Witness* a long or short one?" I asked, Penny being the Agatha Christie expert.

"Long. It's a novel unto itself. One of my favorites," she murmured to Henny, who clucked in agreement.

"So that means you went to bed at…?" I asked Ruth.

She raised an eyebrow again. "You don't honestly think I might have hurt Maya's bird?"

"They asked me for an alibi, too," Alice said.

"Who died and made you detective?" Ruth asked rudely.

"Casper," I said succinctly. "Now, what time were you in bed?"

"I fell asleep in my chair toward the end of the episode, if you must know."

"How could you fall asleep watching David Suchet?" Penny asked. "I think he's the best rendition of Poirot I've ever seen!"

"No one beats Albert Finney in *Murder on the Orient Express*," argued Ruth.

"I disagree. I quite like the version of *Death on the Nile* with Peter Ustinov," said Alice.

Gag, I thought. "No one competes with David Suchet. End of story." I turned to Ruth, eager to end this pointless debate. "Were you watching alone?"

"Alone? Why, yes, of course I was alone. My birds don't sleep inside with me, like some." Ruth pointedly looked at Henny.

I bit back a snort. It didn't even occur to Ruth that she might have a friend over to watch something with her. She'd told me quite bluntly when she moved onto our property that she'd rather not be asked to take on a roommate at any future date. Ever since her husband's death, her ducks had been enough for her.

"Now, now, Ruth," Alice said, pushing her glasses up again. "I know for certain I've seen ducks inside your home before."

Ruth frowned at Alice, but then seemed to brighten. "Ah, you mean my *stuffed* birds."

Penny nearly choked, Henny clucked in surprise, and my jaw dropped.

"You stuff your birds?" I asked, horrified.

"Yes," said Ruth unconcernedly, like stuffing her loved ones was a normal thing to do. I hoped she didn't have her husband lying about somewhere like a mummy…

"Why do you look so shocked?" Alice asked. "It's perfectly normal for people to stuff birds."

"It's also perfectly 'normal' for people to stuff turkeys for dinner, but none of us have ever eaten birds since becoming OBSers." I whirled about the room, daring someone to contradict me. "Right?"

I suddenly realized I'd just assumed the other ladies on our land felt the same way about eating birds as Penny and I did. Our family had stopped eating chicken the day Penny connected with the first Henny and she became her best friend. To do so would have sent Penny off the deep end. We didn't eat meat of any kind. Nor did we stuff our feathered friends once they'd gone on to a better place. It just seemed so…macabre.

"I'm sorry you seem offended," Ruth said, though she didn't sound sorry in the least, "but I'm afraid I do stuff my ducks when they pass. I use a local man, Joseph, down at the hardware store. He's very kind and gentle. Even let me watch once."

Penny gulped beside me and her eyes bulged. I suddenly realized she was about to lose her lunch at the image of watching a taxidermist at work.

But a thought had just occurred to me that distracted my own stomach from revolting.

"You've watched him do it?" I reached into my pocket for the pins. I pulled out the hatpin first, and both Alice and Ruth leaned in closer.

"Is that what did it?" Alice asked, adjusting her glasses for a better look.

"Yes, but I'm more interested in hearing if either of you have ever seen…these before." I pulled out the two smaller pins.

Ruth immediately began to nod. "Naturally. Those are taxidermy pins."

{ 11 }

In Which We Learn the Latin Name for a Duck

Penny and I excused ourselves quickly, thanking Alice and Ruth for their assistance. Penny's grip on Henny was quite tight as we made our way down the road, back toward town.

"You are not allowed to visit Ruth anymore," Penny told her chicken, who seemed to be nodding enthusiastically in agreement.

"We really should have a questionnaire for people who want to move onto our land," Penny said, her brow furrowed at me as though Ruth's habits were my fault.

I didn't disagree, however, as I'd been thinking the same thing. "We should also be a little more thorough in our background checks," I said. "I'm still convinced Casper's death has something to do with Maya's theater history."

"Beatrice also has theater history," Penny pointed out.

"And they're the two that apparently hate each other." I marched with long strides. "Perhaps this all has something to do with the stage?"

"We are about to question a hardware store owner," said Penny.

"And a taxidermist."

Penny shivered.

I know some people may have thought us a little reactionary when it came to our birds, but I didn't hear a lot of folks rushing out to stuff their dead dogs anytime soon. I'm just saying.

The bell above the store door tinkled as we entered, but no one called out a greeting.

Just one of the many reasons why I usually drove almost an hour away to Bedford to do my hardware shopping. My schoolfriend Lou owned the store there, since he'd been unable to get the old codger who'd owned the Paca Springs one since the 18th century to sell to him.

The rows of shelves lined with equipment large and small didn't seem to be hiding anyone. The door behind the counter opened on an empty back room, and the place was eerily silent.

So silent, in fact, that I could hear one of the pins drop as I reached into my pocket to pull out the ones we were going to show Joseph.

Thankfully, I was able to spot the hatpin before it rolled away, the floor being surprisingly clean for a hardware store. The friendly smell of dirt and sawdust must've been wafting in from a side room where more farm-like items were found.

But still no sign of the owner.

If the service was always this bad, I wasn't about to change to the local store.

I leaned over the counter and tapped the bell that was sitting there a couple times, calling out, "Hello? Hello!"

Suddenly, the bell behind us tinkled again as someone else entered the store. He was tall, at least my age, and ruggedly handsome in that Harrison Ford kind of way, wearing a red-and-yellow flannel shirt and jeans, his work boots clomping as he made his way directly toward the counter where we stood. In his hands he carried a small pigeon who wasn't making any sounds, but fluttered slightly, trying to escape his clutches.

The man circled the counter like he owned the place, but it wasn't till he said, "Be with you in just a moment," that I realized he did. I wondered what had happened to the old codger. Maybe this was his son?

He carried the pigeon into the back and we heard some scraping and banging sounds, and then no more fluttering.

When the man returned, he was wiping his hands on a ragged towel.

Both my and Penny's eyes flew up, no doubt meeting the white hairs on our heads.

"Oh my gosh," Penny cried, her hand covering her mouth while the other squished Henny tightly, causing her to cluck in alarm.

"What have you done?" I cried, ready to forget my age, climb over the counter, and hit him with a hammer.

"Woah, woah, woah, ladies," the man said, raising his large hands in defense. "What seems to be the matter here?"

"Did you just kill that bird?!" Penny shouted as I cried, "Do you just help yourself to roadkill whenever you like?!"

"Woah, now, time out, ladies," the man said calmly, his brow furrowed in confusion. "I think there's been a misunderstanding."

"Oh, I don't think so. We know what you do for a living!" I said.

The man quirked his mouth and looked around the store with raised eyebrows. "I think it's pretty obvious to everyone what I do for a living."

"We mean your side hobby!" Penny shouted. I'd never heard her so angry.

"My side hobby?" he asked. "All right, I think we better start over."

"Yes, I think we'd best," I said. "Where were you last night? Out preparing your next victim?"

"Victim?" The man scratched his head. "Now I'm completely lost."

"Did you kill Casper the Whistling Cockatiel?"

At Casper's name, the man's face went white. "Casper's dead?"

"Yes. And I think it's quite clear you're the local bird killer." I placed the pins on the counter and pointed. "Recognize these?"

The hardware store owner leaned forward. "Well, yeah, they look like taxidermy pins." He looked up quickly, then from my face to Penny's and back. "Woah, there, now. You don't think—"

"I just said what we think." I crossed my arms.

"Does Maya know?"

My arms dropped and Penny's head cocked.

"Of course she knows Casper's dead." I waved toward the door. "She's the one that found him."

The man shook his head and sighed. "Poor Maya." Then he looked up and slapped down the towel. "I've got to go to her."

"Woah, woah, woah!" I mimicked him as I blocked his path. He was a big guy, but I was about as tall as him and full of righteous indignation, so he'd have to be pretty bold to push past me. "Stop right there."

He stopped in his tracks. "Please. She'll be so distraught. Maya's my friend."

"You're her friend and you killed her bird?" Penny asked, squeezing Henny tightly.

"No!" he said.

"No, you're not her friend, or no, you didn't kill her bird?" I asked.

"The second," he said. "I didn't kill her bird."

"Really?"

"Of course not. I'd never hurt a bird! I'm a bird lover."

"Coulda fooled me," I said. "What with that bird you just killed so you could stuff it."

"What?" he asked, confusion written all across his face.

"We just watched you walk in with a bird, and we know you're a taxidermist. Ruth told us," I explained.

"Ruth?" he asked.

I was getting real tired of repeating myself. "Yes, Ruth. Ruth Collingwood. You know: the duck lady."

A light went on behind his eyes. "Oh!" he said. "Ruth. Yeah, I know Ruth. I just finished a Canvasback for her. *Aythya valisineria.*"

"Aytha-what-now?" I asked, my turn to be confused.

"*Aythya valisineria*. The Canvasback duck. Order *anseriformes*, family *anatidae*."

"Jiminy cricket," Penny muttered. "You really are a bird lover."

"Absolutely I am. Which is why I'd never hurt a bird, much less one that belonged to a dear friend of mine." He blushed slightly.

"Dear friend, eh? And does this dear friend know about your tendency to collect dead birds off the side of the road to add to your taxidermy collection?"

"What are you—" Again, the light. "Oh! The pigeon!" He held up a finger. "Wait just one second."

He turned around and went into the back room. After only a moment he returned carrying an open-topped box. He set it on the countertop and beckoned me and Penny closer.

"Come and see," he said.

We both leaned in.

Inside the box was the pigeon—cooing happily and nestled warmly in a collection of old blankets, her right wing wrapped against her body in a splint.

Penny and I both looked up at each other, then at the hardware store man.

"I'm so sorry," Penny apologized first.

"Me, too," I said. "Guess I was wrong."

"Not a problem." He held out his hand to me. "I'm Joseph, by the way."

"Goose," I said.

"Penny," my sister said. "And this is Henny." She held up Henny's wing in a wave.

"Nice to meet you," Joseph said. "Now if you don't mind, would you tell me what happened to Casper?"

{ 12 }

In Which We Discover Steampunk

Joseph shook his head sadly as we finished our tale of Casper's demise. Then he leaned forward and picked up one of the smaller pins.

"I understand what brought you here. These do look like taxidermy pins. There's no way of knowing whose they are, though."

"May we ask again what you were doing last night, but nicely?" I asked with a smile.

Joseph smiled in return. He had a kind, friendly smile. One that invited confidences. "I'm afraid I don't have much of an alibi. I go to bed pretty early these days." He scratched the stubble on his chin, which still grew in dark though his hair was a thick smoky-gray. "Gotta make it to the Tavern for my morning coffee and town gossip."

The Tavern was officially named the Washington and Jefferson Town Tavern, but as it was the only place for coffee and breakfast starting at five a.m., most Paca Springs folks just called it "the Tavern." Aunt Connie had declared once that she knew when she opened the Quaint Quail it was no use competing for the early birds, so she opened at eight instead. These days it was an even split, though, between who breakfasted at the Quail vs. the Tavern.

Neither of them caught me. I was a strict home-breakfaster, as I preferred eating my first meal of the day in my pajamas and slippers.

"If you don't mind my saying, you seemed pretty eager to see Maya when we told you the news," I said, recalling his reference to his "dear friend." "As far as I know, Maya's only been in town a couple months or so. How do you know her?"

Again, Joseph blushed. "We're just good friends. She came into the shop when she first moved into town and we got to talking about music and such."

"You're familiar with show tunes?" Penny asked in surprise. I, too, hadn't figured a hardware store man for the type who'd like musicals.

But Joseph was nodding enthusiastically. "I grew up doing local theater. Not acting, mind you, but backstage. I'm helping with the *Wizard of Oz* production right now."

Penny and I exchanged a glance.

"Oh," I said. "So you know Beatrice, then?"

Again his cheeks and neck reddened. This man was a regular horse of many colors.

"I've been helping some with the costume design, inasmuch as Beatrice requests my assistance. Haven't seen or heard from her in a week."

"Oh?" I asked, raising my brows.

"Yeah. Early on, though, we were working pretty closely, seeing as this particular production is being done in a steampunk theme." Joseph scratched the back of his head. "I'd never heard of 'steampunk' till I started helping with this production."

"Neither have I," Penny said. "What is it?"

"It's difficult to explain. Beatrice said, 'Just imagine if Victorians had taken steam power to the next level, like to the point of creating computers or airplanes. What would that look like?' It's Victorian-era costuming, but anachronistic because it's been mixed with space-age technology."

"I'm still confused." Penny's brow furrowed.

"Are you familiar with the *Back to the Future* movies?"

"Of course," we said in unison.

"All right then, the last scene in the third *Back to the Future* movie where Doc Brown appears with the flying steam engine time machine? That's steampunk. There just hasn't been a name for it till now."

I raised a brow.

"Here, it's easier if I show you."

Joseph picked up the box with the pigeon inside and returned it to the back room. When he reappeared, he had a large contraption in his hands. It looked like an old vacuum cleaner painted bronze with straps hanging from the cylinder. Gears and watch faces and pressure dials were gathered at the top, where two exhaust pipes reached for the sky.

"What the?" I said.

But Penny squealed in excitement. "Oh my goodness, is that a jetpack?"

I shot her a quizzical look as Joseph smiled. "You mean like *The Rocketeer*?" I asked.

"Exactly! It's for one of the flying monkeys."

"Of course it is!" Penny said, practically jumping up and down in excitement. Henny was mimicking my look of concern. "Oooo! I can't wait to see this show now!" She looked at me with that crazed grin. "Why aren't you more excited by this? Victorians are *your* thing."

"Yeah, Victorians. Not science fiction."

"Excuse me, but what about H.G. Wells or Jules Verne? Didn't they write Victorian science fiction?"

"In fact, they're both perfect examples of steampunk," Joseph said, scratching his chin. "Phileas Fogg would've loved something like this for his journey around the world in eighty days. And H.G. Wells practically invented the genre with *The Time Machine*."

"Huh...," I murmured.

I considered the jetpack. Flying monkeys with jetpacks instead of wings? And I'd seen the costumes already in Beatrice's front room. Lots of corsets and petticoats and vests and top hats and goggles.

"So, where do the peacock feathers come in?" I asked, recalling the color scheme.

"I take it you've seen the costumes. Beatrice is naturally going with a peacock Emerald City look," Joseph said with a shrug. "What else would you expect from her?"

I nodded in acknowledgement. "All right, but we're getting off topic here. What does this all have to do with Maya? Is she helping with the show, too?"

"Not that I'm aware of." Joseph shook his head. "Unless she's been helping Beatrice with costumes, but somehow I doubt that." He rubbed the back of his neck and became very interested in the straps on the jetpack. "Those two don't seem to get along very well."

Another person who'd noticed. How had I missed this? Was I really that unaware of the underlying tensions building on our land? It was a hazard to our way of life, really. We couldn't have ladies who hated each other living in such close proximity for the rest of their lives.

In fact, I wondered at Maya's wish to rent a house on our land, if this problem with Beatrice had been building for so long. Beatrice had not only been my friend since our school days, she'd gone on to be my roommate in college; coming from a small town, we'd clung to each other that first semester like two fresh ducklings going for their first swim. There was no way I would be asking Beatrice to move out over Maya, a woman I barely knew.

Unless she was a murderer.

If Beatrice killed Casper, I'd have to rethink those convictions.

Until I knew for certain, I wasn't going to push anyone out, but I'd definitely be having a good long talk with both of them in the near future. Maybe a mediation was in order.

"Why do you think that is?" Penny asked, bringing me back to the moment at hand.

Joseph blushed. But before I could ask straight out if it had anything to do with him or the show, the bell above his door rang.

And his face turned even redder.

{ 13 }

In Which the First Day Finally Ends and Another Begins

Maya's face matched Joseph's as she tried to melt into the floor.

"Maya!" I cried with a smile.

Her hand still grasped the door handle like a lifeline. "I just forgot, I have to—"

I crossed the intervening space in two steps and put my arm around her shoulder, stopping her from leaving. "We were just talking about you!" I said happily.

"I heard about Casper," Joseph said to Maya's feet. "I'm so sorry."

Maya studied Joseph's counter. "Thanks," she said, so softly I think only Henny really heard it.

Thankfully, the interaction alleviated some of the embarrassment that had sent all the blood rushing to both their faces, so we wouldn't be dealing with any fainters.

"Joseph here was showing us some of his work for the *Wizard of Oz*," I said, waving to the jetpack. "Have you helped with the production at all? I was just wondering why Casper wasn't invited to whistle a solo for the show. It was kind of his thing, wasn't it?"

Maya shook her head.

"Were you looking for something?" Joseph asked.

"What?" Maya looked up, met his eyes, then quickly looked away again.

"I just wondered if there was something I could help you with."

Maya shook her head. "No...nothing. I'll be going." And she turned on her heel and shot out the door before any of us could stop her.

"Thanks for your help, Joseph," Penny said, shaking his hand. "I think we better walk Maya home. She seems a little lost."

I shook Joseph's hand, too, apologized again for the rude introduction, and followed Penny and Henny out the door.

Maya had slowed outside. It only took a few long strides for me to catch up to her, while Penny ran to join the two of us.

"I'm sorry, Maya," I said, figuring an apology would soften her up. "You can go back if you want. We're all done now if you wanted to talk to your friend."

"He's not my friend," she muttered. "I mean, he is, but...he..."

"He's more than a friend, isn't he?" Penny said softly, and Henny clucked in consensus.

Maya's cheeks reddened to match the setting sun on the horizon. Hard to believe the day was ending already, though in some ways it had also been a terribly long day. Especially for Maya.

"He's...well...I thought he might be. But he's not."

She didn't have to say it. Penny and I both knew it. I felt like I should voice it just to be sure, though.

"Beatrice?" I asked.

Maya's lips tightened, her fists balled at her sides. "I thought he might finally be the one. I mean, I know I'm turning sixty this year, but I always thought maybe...someday..."

"Joseph seems like a real nice guy," I said.

Maya nodded and smiled a little. "He is."

"I mean, other than the fact that he likes to stuff birds in his free time," I muttered. I've never been good at biting my tongue.

Maya stopped walking. "What?"

Penny and I stopped, too, and faced her. I looked at Penny, who shrugged like I might as well keep going, since my foot was already in my mouth. "Penny and I just learned from Ruth that she gets her ducks stuffed when they pass. And Joseph's the guy that does the stuffing."

"Like, a taxidermist?" Maya asked.

"Yeah," I said slowly.

I could see Maya working through the information, her eyebrows making an angry "V" shape over her eyes. Then she nodded and started walking again.

Penny raised a brow at me and I shrugged before we started walking, too.

"I'm going to bury Casper tonight," Maya said. I thought her comment completely non sequitur until I realized she'd probably gotten there after deciding she wouldn't be stuffing the poor guy.

Penny and I nodded.

"We'd like to be there," Penny said.

But Maya shook her head. "No, thank you. I need to do this alone."

I hoped I hadn't offended her by my comment, and I eventually said so.

Maya waved her hand, but didn't stop her march back toward the house. "It's all right. I just want to say goodbye in my own way. We've been through a lot together, Casper and me. I want to finish this right."

Penny hugged Henny tightly enough to produce a soft cluck. "We understand," she said softly.

When we reached the house, we parted ways: Maya headed for her room, Penny and I headed for the kitchen.

Neither of us felt incredibly hungry, however, so we just sat at the table with a couple cups of lemonade, some apple slices, and chunks of cheese as we considered the day. Before long, we heard Maya coming back down the stairs and out the door, the slamming of the screen door resounding through the foyer.

"I suppose I should've pointed her toward the graveyard," Penny said softly, her hand restlessly petting Henny at her side.

I shook my head. "Nah. That graveyard's personal. She needs to find her own place to bury her bird. Someplace that meant something to the two of them."

Penny nodded, no doubt happy I'd voiced aloud what she'd really been thinking herself.

Soon after we said good night, making sure the front porch lights were left on for Maya before turning in. I grabbed the copy of *The Prestige* Sable had lent me as I climbed into bed, grateful for the distraction.

Although the story began in the present day with many intriguing references to mysterious occurrences, it then switched to a memoir written by Alfred Borden in 1901, recounting the events that comprised his career as a stage magician. I was soon lost amidst the dazzle of the late 19th century's fascination with illusionists, all the while keeping my eyes open for the twist Sable had said I'd never see coming. Which meant I was up much too late reading...

I awoke with a jolt the next morning to the sound of that blasted peacock yelping on our rooftop.

"Shut up!" I yelled at the ceiling, pulling my pillow over my head. When I finally looked at the clock, though, I realized the peacock was right, and I should've been up by now. It was almost nine o'clock! The events of the day before must've done me in more than I'd realized.

As I made my way downstairs, I recalled my rather vivid dream of the night before. Something to do with a spiritualist in a cabinet trying to convince me he was communicating with Casper on the Other Side. But I'd been on to his chicanery and so I'd left my place in the circle of linked hands to fling open the cabinet doors, prepared to reveal the truth of the illusion. Only to find Casper inside, "whistling a happy tune" from *The King and I*.

Slings and Sparrows

I wasn't surprised to find that Penny had already left for our normal Sunday morning church service at the local Methodist chapel on the corner. One of the perks of living in the same town we'd grown up in was that people didn't turn up their noses when Penny started bringing a chicken to church with her. It also didn't hurt that the current pastor was married to our cousin Joanna, one of Aunt Connie's brood. His family had even gone so far as to create a Henny greeting box in the back of the sanctuary, so if anyone wanted to say hi afterward they could do so, before shaking his own hand at the door.

Some days, however, Penny and I worshipped in what our dad would call "God's cathedral," meaning nature, and I was feeling like this was more my speed today, given I highly doubted I'd be able to focus on anything Pastor Jeremiah was saying.

My Sunday morning routine was interrupted, however, when I almost dropped the entire gallon of milk into my bowl of cereal. Someone was *whistling*.

Visions of ghostly white cockatiels filled my head.

I followed the sound into the sunroom.

Thank God, it wasn't Casper.

It was Maya.

{ 14 }

In Which We Discuss Peacocks

"It's a miracle!" I cried.

Maya whirled around, a look of absolute surprise on her face. "Goose? What are you doing here?"

"Sorry," I said, my hands raised in defense. I'd been surprising people a lot lately, it seemed.

"I thought I heard you and Penny leave for church."

"Yeah, Penny did, but I decided to stay back this morning. Sorry I scared you."

"It's all right." Maya's face settled into a more normal look. "I just hadn't realized...I thought I was alone."

I looked around, just to be certain there wasn't a cockatiel back from the dead. "But...that was *you* whistling?"

Maya blushed. "Yes."

"Does that mean your voice is healed?" I cried excitedly, wondering why she didn't look happier.

Slings and Sparrows

Maya sat down in a wicker chair. "I've always been able to whistle. Never lost that. It's the singing—that's what changed."

"You've always been able to whistle?"

"Well, yeah, how do you think I taught Casper to whistle?" she asked sardonically, her brows and tone of voice in a "duh" formation. "But you're right. I have gotten better. It's been steadily getting better for a couple months now."

Good timing, I thought. With the loss of Casper, and with him her livelihood, she would need to consider alternative sources of income—unless she'd saved or invested her earnings wisely through the years. I didn't feel like now was a good time to question her financial sense, though.

"That's great!" I said, again sounding much happier than she did. "You'll be able to return to the stage! Just like Casper would have wanted."

Maya sighed and studied the empty birdcage hanging in the corner. "Perhaps…perhaps I might be able to…whistle some of his favorite tunes. In memoriam."

"I'm sure his fans would appreciate that," I said, then wondered if he had any. The way Maya had talked about their career yesterday, she'd made it sound like they were a worldwide sensation.

"Perhaps you could start with joining the local production of *Wizard of Oz*? Maybe whistle an opening song or closing song or something?"

Maya actually scoffed at my suggestion.

"What?" I said. "Why is that such a bad idea?"

"I'm sorry," said Maya, "but you just don't get it, do you? You actually *like* Beatrice."

Beatrice again.

"Yes, I do," I said, a bit snippily, I'm afraid. I was getting a little fed up with the "woe is me, your friend is a killer" act.

Maya seemed surprised to hear me say it out loud. So I kept going.

"Beatrice is a sweet, wonderful person, and she's completely harmless." I waved my hand. "She just likes to ruffle her feathers and show off."

Maya scoffed. "Well, she certainly puts on quite the show."

I crossed my arms. I was honking mad now. "I've known Beatrice since we were ten, but I know nothing about *you*. Of course I'm going to trust Beatrice over you. Prove to me why I shouldn't trust her over someone I know nothing about."

"Because she *stole* the *one man* I've ever *loved*!" Maya shouted, rising from her chair and pointing out the sunroom like Joseph was standing there, blushing and smiling at her.

I rocked back. I knew it. I knew this was about a man. It's always about men with Beatrice. When would she ever learn?

But I couldn't say that aloud. I had to defend her and her stupid actions. I was her friend for crying out loud. Her stupidly loyal friend.

"Listen, she probably doesn't even realize she hurt you. She probably has no idea you're mad at her. In fact, I know she has no idea."

"How?"

"'Cause I asked her!" I yelled. "That's what friends do. They *talk* to each other. Jiminy crickets, this isn't a Jane Austen novel. She told me she hadn't a clue why you'd be mad at her."

"Yes. She. Does," Maya said through gritted teeth. "She has to. How could she be so completely unaware?"

It was my turn to scoff. "Have you met Beatrice? If he's male and has two legs—nope, even that's debatable, 'cause there was that guy last summer with the peg leg—the point is: if he's male, she knows nothing but that she's gotta ruffle her feathers and display."

"It's the peacock that does that, not the peahen."

"So she's a little confused!" I shouted. I threw up my hands and let out a frustrated, "Ugh!" Maybe Tomi and Tuppence were more frustrated with life than I'd realized, given how often I'd heard them make that same sound.

"How can you think that's okay?" Maya asked. "I like Joseph, and I thought he liked me, too. Then along comes Beatrice, 'displaying' as you put it, and suddenly I'm nobody to him. They had dinner together, and the next day when I saw him, he could barely look me in the face. It's not hard to put two and two together. Especially where Beatrice is concerned."

I bit my lip. She might be right. "But she told me she's with Billy Bacon," I said, my tone a little softer than a second ago.

Maya rolled her eyes. "You said it yourself: with her it just has to be male. She obviously had her fun with Joseph, then moved on to the next big thing."

"When?"

"When what?"

"When were Beatrice and Joseph together?"

Maya avoided my eyes and muttered something.

"What?"

"A couple weeks ago," she said a little clearer.

"A couple weeks?" I threw up my hands. "That's like a year to Beatrice. No wonder she doesn't remember."

"Well," said Maya, and I realized tears were forming in her eyes, "I do."

Once I saw the tears coming, I got out of there fast. No way was I going to deal with an angry-crying Maya. Sad-crying was bad enough.

I took off out the door, not caring where my feet took me.

Perhaps not too surprisingly, they took me to Beatrice's.

Outside her house, I found a peacock displaying for a peahen, turning to shake his bare tail feathers at her while the extended colored feathers made a soft whirring sound reminiscent of a rattlesnake.

Or perhaps it was more like a sewing machine.

There was no response to my knock at the door, so I let myself in to the loud whirring tornado that was Beatrice's last-minute attempt to complete her costumes. I couldn't see if she'd made any headway, since as far as I could tell, the mess of costume bits and pieces were still all over the couch, chairs, hanging from the ceiling, and covering every possible surface. I also counted three or four illustrated versions of *The Wizard of Oz* novel. I wondered how many times Beatrice had read the book seeking inspiration for her costumes.

"Beatrice!" I shouted. "Beatrice!" But it took me placing a hand on her shoulder for her to squeal just like she had for Maya the day before.

"Good heavenly days! You've got to stop doing that!" she cried, her hand to her chest. "What, Goose? Can't you see I'm up to my eyeballs in work?"

"We need to talk," I said calmly and firmly.

Beatrice removed her sewing glasses and let them hang from a chain about her neck. "Oh, dear. It must be serious."

I took a deep breath and started to sit down, only then realizing there was nowhere to sit. So I stood and took another breath, trying real hard to think through my words before I began.

"Beatrice, you've done it again."

"I have?" she asked, her voice indicating she'd taken it as a compliment.

"No, I mean: you've done it again," I repeated, this time changing my emphasis and lowering my voice, attempting to reveal she was in trouble, not getting an award.

"Goose, I don't have time for guessing games. Get to the point. What have I done?"

"You took Maya's man."

Beatrice's blue-shadowed eyelids flew up to meet her pencil-lined eyebrows, her perfectly red lips curving into an "O."

I nodded. "That's why she's mad at you."

"Oh, dear," she said, shaking her head. Then she cocked a brow at me. "Which one?"

"Ha!" escaped from me before I could stop it. "Really, Beatrice?"

Beatrice made a face and shrugged. "It's not Billy, is it? I'd just hate to give him up..."

"It's not Billy," I said, and before she had a chance to list off a half-dozen others, I delivered the punchline. "It's Joseph."

Beatrice pursed her lips and smiled. "Well, that explains that."

"That explains why Maya is so furious with you she's convinced you went and killed her cockatiel?"

"No!" Beatrice exclaimed. "That explains why Joseph wouldn't even kiss me!"

"Kiss you?"

"Yeah. He practically ran out the door when I leaned in."

"So you and Joseph didn't..." I waved my hand.

"No," Beatrice said with astonishment. "Of course we didn't..." She waved her hand in imitation.

I smiled. "Well, that's good."

"But Maya still obviously thinks we did, for you to come over here all worked up like that."

"Yes, she does."

"But seeing as there was no beginning in the first place..." She replaced her glasses on her nose. "Speaking of which, if that'll be all? I really must get back to work."

I nodded, smiled, and waved goodbye. Beatrice's foot had already returned to the pedal.

Now, I realized I'd just taken my friend's word that there was nothing more to the story, but there was a pretty strong foundation of trust built up between me and Beatrice. She'd helped me through my first heartbreak when my crush didn't ask me to the school dance, taken me to the hospital after my foot broke through the ice in the crick, and covered for me when I'd snuck a cigarette from my uncle's pack to give it a try, knowing full well my dad would have given me a woopin' I'd never forget if he'd cottoned on. When you've got history with someone, that's just the way it goes.

Slings and Sparrows

I also felt sure there had to be more to Maya's backstory than she was letting on.

It was time to search the news.

{ 15 }

In Which We Marvel At Victorian Lit

Now, Penny and I subscribed to *The Paca Springs Gazette*, but if I wanted to learn about Maya, I was going to have to search farther afield, which would require heading into town to the Quaint Quail. I glanced at my watch and realized the café wouldn't even be open yet. On Sunday they didn't open till two, leaving time for church and Sunday lunch with the family.

It was too late to go to church myself, so I headed toward Sable's. She wouldn't be working and she only went to church rarely, being a lapsed Catholic, so she was the most likely person to be available for listening.

I was in luck. When I knocked on the door, Hugin cawed an answer, but it was Sable who opened the door and welcomed me in. I took a seat on her couch and she offered me some tea. I accepted, since Sable made her own better-than-store-bought herbal tea out of her garden-variety herbs and spices.

I sipped the blend of peppermint and marshmallow root—as well as other things, but those were the only two my unrefined tastebuds could pick out—in contentment as Sable slid out a chair to join me.

"I started *The Prestige* last night," I said.

"And?"

"And it's intriguing. I think it would make a fantastic movie. I feel like a lot of the tricks in it are visual. His descriptions make me want to see them done in real life."

"Don't say anything more till you've finished it, then," said Sable. "I don't want to give away by my facial expressions whether your predictions are right or wrong."

I tipped my head to her. "Understandable. I will say, though, that the whole book feels like a magic trick. The memoir by Alfred Borden even says as much up front—says he'll be opening, like all magicians, by showing he has nothing up his sleeve, though of course I know he must have something hidden there..."

Sable just sipped her tea.

"All right, all right, I'll stop now."

"Have you figured out your real-life mystery yet?" Sable asked, smoothly changing the subject.

"No, though I did solve the question of why Maya and Beatrice are at odds."

"Let me guess: a man."

I nodded. "That one was too easy."

"It's not that Billy Bacon character is it? He doesn't seem like Maya's type. But I may be wrong."

"No, it's the new hardware store owner: Joseph something."

"Joseph Hollister. He's not 'new'—he's run the local store for the past year at least."

"Really?"

"Yeah, though I suppose that's 'new' by Paca Springs standards."

I raised a brow at her. "You know him?"

Sable gave a slight smile. "I went to school with him. I was friends with his younger sister."

"So you know him pretty well?"

She shrugged. "As well as anyone knows their friend's older brother." Was that a slight hint of red in her cheeks I detected?

"Did you know he's a taxidermist?"

"You say that like it's a bad thing."

I set down my cup. "How is it Penny and I are the only two who seem to have a problem with it?"

Sable quirked a brow. "Why would you have a problem with it? It's a very normal thing for a bird lover to do. I'll probably have Hugin stuffed when he goes. Might get him a motion-activated voice box, too, so he can scare the bejeebers out of whoever comes to my door."

"Nevermore," he croaked on cue from his perch near my head, making me grateful I'd already set down my cup so it didn't end up in pieces on the floor.

"'Deep into that darkness peering,'" I quoted, "'long I stood there wondering, fearing, / Doubting, dreaming dreams no mortal ever dared to dream before; / But the silence was unbroken, and the stillness gave no token, / And the only word there spoken was the whispered word—'"

"Nevermore," croaked Hugin.

Slings and Sparrows

"I don't think that's your line just yet," I said. "You've got at least three stanzas to go before you appear."

"She's right, you know," Sable said to her raven.

"Nevermore," he croaked again.

"Let me guess: that's the first thing you ever taught him to speak?"

Sable grinned. "You'd think that, but no. First I tried to teach him the words to my favorite poem, 'Jabberwocky.'"

I chuckled. "''Twas brillig, and the slithy toves / Did gyre and gimble in the wabe: / All mimsy were the borogoves, / And the mome raths outgrabe.'"

"Precisely. But the words were too difficult for him."

"They're too difficult for *me*. I'm the Victorian lit prof and I still haven't the slightest idea what the poem's about."

"I've always figured that's precisely the point of *Alice* in general. That's why I like it: it ridicules the education system of the time and remarks on how none of the things we think are important in life really are. It's not meant to make sense."

"Much like the murder of Casper."

"You haven't a clue who shot him?"

"My money's on a sparrow with a bow and arrow," I said, thinking of the old children's rhyme about Cock Robin.

"Oh, to suffer the slings of bows and arrows of outrageous fortune!" Sable parodied as she poured herself some more tea, showing off her black-painted fingernails that I joked she used to hide the dirt. "Too bad we've no sparrows in the OBS, eh?"

"Yeah."

"You know, I've just realized how much we all emulate our birds," Sable said with a smile and a glance toward Hugin in his corner. "It's like that scene at the beginning of the cartoon *101 Dalmatians* where each of the owners walks by with a dog that looks just like them."

"Are you saying I'm a loud-mouthed, honking, gabbling goose?" I laughed. "Yep, that about sums me up!"

Sable chuckled, but given the way she currently sat stooped over her cup of tea dressed all in black, I had to admit, she had a point.

I proffered my cup when Sable asked if I wanted more. "I just can't bring myself to suspect the other ladies in the OBS, though."

"Really? How well do you actually know everyone?" Sable asked. "People usually kill in books over something selfish. Money, fame, lust. Something someone else has that they don't. Jealousy."

"Jealousy of the fame Maya had accomplished through Casper?" I suggested.

"Jealousy of a man Maya took from her?" Sable suggested in return.

I waved the thought off. "I've already dismissed Beatrice from suspicion."

"Oh?" Sable raised an eyebrow. "That's not very good detective work, Goose. You're supposed to keep an open mind."

"Beatrice said they didn't even kiss, and he was the one who left."

"All right, then jealousy of a man Maya *kept* from her? Beatrice might not have liked being passed over for someone else."

"Why does everyone have it out for Beatrice?" I asked, exasperatedly. "You've known her nearly as long as I have."

Slings and Sparrows

Beatrice, Sable, and I had been the Three Musketeers since meeting our junior year of college, though Sable was three years younger than us. It had turned out, in one of those crazy small-world coincidences, that Sable was from the little town of Chambersburg not far from Paca Springs, and we'd been friends ever since.

The point was, Sable knew what Beatrice was like, and, therefore, should have a little more sympathy for her. Right?

"I don't have it out for her," Sable said, setting down her cup. "It's just that the only clue you have seems to point directly to her."

I sighed. I couldn't argue with that.

A glance at the clock told me it was a little past one. Time to head to the Quaint Quail.

{ 16 }

In Which We Learn I'm Not a Goose

By the time I reached Aunt Connie's, the place was packed with the after-church crowd, but I was able to catch Jackie's eye from where I stood along the wall.

"You here for lunch, Goose?" she asked.

I shook my head. "Don't mind me. I was just going to sneak into the back to look at some of your newspapers. You wouldn't happen to keep older back issues would you?"

Jackie laughed. "If Mom had anything to say about it, we'd rent a shed just so she could keep more of them. 'You never know when they might come in handy,' she always says. She'll be thrilled to know someone can use them. Come on."

I followed her into the back hallway that was the secret sanctum beyond the kitchen.

"They're in this closet here," she said, leading me past the restrooms to a closet across from the office, where she peeked her head in.

"Yinz all right in here, Juliette?" she asked her daughter.

Jules smiled and nodded, her mouth full of food. "Heya, Goose!" She gave a hello nod to me with her hands full of sandwich, her eyebrows rising toward the top of her perfectly smooth close-shaved head. She was a recent breast cancer survivor, and with her darker skin tone being closer to Beatrice's than mine, she looked like a warrior princess—which she was.

"Hey, Jules!" I said warmly. Then I smiled at the two little ones seated at a miniature table, placed there for the express purpose of Aunt Connie's great-grandkids.

Nicole looked up at me with bright, inquisitive eyes. "You're not a goose," she said, quite accurately.

Thus far, I'd only had the pleasure of meeting the kids in passing while they scurried about at family gatherings. It was funny to realize that this was, apparently, Nicole's first introduction to my name.

"You're very observant," I said.

I'd always had a hard time talking to young children. Once they were eight or older, then I could usually find a common ground, like discussing books with them. But before then, it was hard to know what to say.

"She's not a goose, she's just old," said Chris, the ever-more-knowledgeable big brother.

"Chris!" his mother admonished in That Tone of Voice.

"It's all right," I said to Jules before turning to Chris. "Right again. And how old do you think I am?"

The boy screwed up his face for a moment, then answered decisively, "Twenty-seven."

"Right *again*! You're on fire!" I said, giving him a high-five for uplifting my spirits. Perhaps young kids could serve a purpose after all.

"So what's up?" Jules asked, wiping her mouth.

The plate in front of her that had been full five seconds ago was now empty. Young moms knew how to eat fast. It's like they were always looking for the quickest way to fill their bellies so they could get back to helping their kids with whatever emergency they were involved in next.

With a four- and six-year-old, I imagined those emergencies were often hot on the heels of one another.

"Goose wanted to look at Mom's collection of old newspapers," said Jackie.

"Why?" Jules wrinkled her nose.

"I need to look up someone. A performer. I figured with all the subscriptions floating around here, I was bound to find something."

In addition to the local paper, the café subscribed to the *Washington Post*, *Washington City Paper*, *Washington Times*, *Baltimore Sun*, *Philadelphia Inquirer*, *Philadelphia Tribune*, *Pittsburgh Post-Gazette*, *Pittsburgh Tribune*, and the *Pittsburgh City Paper* just to name a few. If Maya was telling the truth, I would no doubt find listings in the theater section of one of those big city papers advertising the performance of Casper the Whistling Cockatiel.

"You know, you could search the internet."

I exchanged a glance with Jackie. "I dunno..."

My son, Derrick, had talked about the internet and email and chat rooms and all that, but most of our friends were local and the only one who wasn't was Derrick himself, who could just as easily call me. When I'd retired as a professor, computers had just started appearing in classrooms; I was glad I'd left before having to learn to use them. Penny and I didn't have a computer at our house, and I didn't have one of those newfangled cellular phones, either. If someone wanted to get ahold of me, they could call the phone at the house. That had been good enough for me for decades, it was good enough now.

"The internet would be so much easier," Jules said.

Jackie shrugged and turned to go back to the kitchen, but first she made a gesture toward me as if to say, "I can't help you anymore, but go with your cousin and she'll see you through." It was amazing how much could be said in a gesture when you were family.

"Flipping through newspapers searching for the mention of a single name is going to take you weeks. Here, let me show you." Jules dusted off her hands and moved her plate to the side, turning in the rolling chair to face the computer. She pushed a switch and the machine's screen powered on. The sound of dialing filled the air and then a scratchy noise that made me jump.

"It's just the computer," Chris said from his seat at the kids' table.

"It's dye-uh-ling," said Nicole confidently.

"Like a phone?" I asked the four-year-old who knew more than me about modern technology.

Nicole looked at her mother, who nodded, then she turned her braided head to me and nodded herself. "Uh huh."

"I see."

Finally the computer stopped screeching and switched to making binging sounds. Then it sat there humming softly like a Canadian goose glowering at me in anticipation.

"Now, who are you looking for?" Jules asked, resting her hands on the keyboard like a pro.

"Just like that?"

"Yep. Just like that. It's called a search engine. This one just launched last month and I love the way it's set up. You just type in your question and it answers it for you. It's called Ask Jeeves."

I snorted. "Like P.G. Wodehouse's valet?"

"I don't know who that is."

I almost choked on my own intake of breath. "You don't know who Jeeves is?"

"Um, no." Jules shrugged. "Sorry. I take it he's someone from a Victorian novel?"

I shook my head. "No, they're books from the 1920s and '30s."

"Hold on," said Jules, and I watched her type in, *Who is Jeeves?*, into the computer. After a minute or two, the screen filled with a bunch of underlined blue words. "Here we go." Jules clicked on the top listing and we were taken to another page. "Apparently, the Jeeves novels feature Bertie Wooster, and were published starting in 1919 until 1974."

My jaw dropped.

"Pretty impressive, right?" Jules asked.

"Ask it why the sky is blue!" cried Nicole.

"Ask it why chicken salad has celery in it!" suggested Chris, who then muttered, "I don't like celery."

"You'll learn to like it," said Jules, without even turning to her son. "Right now, Cousin Goose needs to ask it some questions, okay?" She turned to me again. "Type any subject into Ask Jeeves and it'll bring up links from around the world concerning that subject."

I took a step back. "That is *so* dangerous."

"No it's not, it's the information age. At the tips of my fingers is everything I'll ever need to learn. I could research anything in ten minutes that used to take yinz weeks to look up."

I realized then how much I'd missed out on. Apparently during my absence from the world, shows like *Star Trek* had become reality.

"So," Jules asked, wriggling her eyebrows at me, "is it a man you want to check out?"

"Psh," I said in response, for that was the only way to respond to that kind of joke. "Nah, something else." I glanced toward the kids. "I can fill you in later."

She nodded, getting my drift, and beckoned for me to take a seat and pull myself closer to the computer desk. I did so and she leaned over and asked softly, "What are you looking for?"

"I want to look up Maya Grove and her cockatiel, Casper."

"The dead bird and your newest roommate?" Jules asked. Apparently Aunt Connie had filled in her family for me.

I nodded.

"Looking for anything in particular?"

"Just some background info. I know next to nothing about her except what she's told me, and I want to find out how much of that is accurate."

"You think she might've been on the run or something?"

I shrugged. "Maybe. Won't know till the internets tells me." I waved a hand toward the computer screen.

"All right, well, let's just try a basic search first, and see what that gets you. If you're looking for something more specific, you might ask a librarian to help. They've got a row of computers now and seem to be pretty knowledgeable when I go to them with questions."

"I'm trying to keep this on the down low," I said, well aware that this was one of those phrases that aged me when I was around people like Jules.

Not Jules herself—Jules never made me feel old—but people as young as Jules. And yes, thirty wasn't that young to some people, but Aunt Connie would swear up and down that she was still young at eighty-five, so who knows? In the end, maybe Beatrice was on to something when she said, "You're only as old as you think you are."

"Momma, can we go outside?" Chris whined.

"Pull the whine out and throw it away," said Jules.

"Momma, can we please go outside?" Chris asked again, but I noticed that this time he had definitely pulled back on the whininess. Score one for Mom.

"All right, give me two minutes," she said to him, then turned back to me. "I've gotta give these kids some outdoor time," Jules said apologetically. "Do you think you could get started on your own at least? Here..." She clicked in the little box where she'd typed her question. "What was the bird's stage name?"

"Casper the Whistling Cockatiel."

Jules nodded and typed, *Who is Casper the Whistling Cockatiel?*

She clicked the search button and a bunch of new underlined blue words appeared. "There you go. Now just go through and click the links that sound like what you want and click this button here when you want to go to the next page. It's just like flipping through the pages of a newspaper. That should keep you busy for a little while."

"Thanks, you're amazing," I said as Jules rose from her chair.

"Tell my kids that, would you?" Jules said with a wink.

{ 17 }

In Which We Learn How To Use the Internet

I waved to the kids as I switched chairs, feeling like I was taking over the helm of a ship without any idea how to steer.

Luckily, it turned out to be quite easy to click and read. And boy, howdy, was there a lot to read.

The web search turned up a lot of interesting information, and I quickly realized I needed to start taking notes, as Penny would surely want to know what I'd uncovered. I grabbed some loose paper from the printer and began jotting things down. I soon found myself heading down a rabbit hole of curiouser and curiouser information as I uncovered just how popular little Casper had been.

Maya hadn't been joking when she'd said they'd performed on the biggest stages across the nation. At the Kennedy Center in D.C., their performances with the symphony had sold out two years in a row. They'd also made cameo appearances in stage productions in Seattle and Chicago, including *The King and I* and *Wizard of Oz*.

It was too bad she and Beatrice were at such odds. Our little town of Paca Springs would've been really fortunate to have Casper and Maya make an appearance in the community theater production. Our stage was the school gym, not exactly the Kennedy Center, but it served its purpose.

I began making a list of all the places they'd performed, but I gave up after it became too long, though I did add tallies to all the biggest places for each performance. They'd been in Philadelphia three times, but there was no mention of performances at the Hagerstown Fairgrounds or anywhere closer to us than the Apollo Civic Theater in Martinsburg, West Virginia, which was a good forty-five minute drive away.

I wondered what had drawn Maya to Paca Springs, if her engagements normally kept her busy elsewhere. It wasn't like we were on a direct train line to D.C. or Baltimore or anything. The only way in and out of Paca Springs was by road, and if it snowed more than a couple inches, or a New England fog came down out of the Appalachians, or someone sneezed too hard in the grocery store, often the roads were closed.

I couldn't find much on Maya herself. It seemed like she hadn't existed outside of being Casper's trainer and human counterpart.

"Have you found any pictures?" someone asked from the doorway.

I turned and discovered I'd been joined by Penny and Alice.

"Juliette told us you were back here researching," Alice continued in that low voice of hers, "so we thought we'd see if we could help."

"Thanks, but I think I'm almost through," I said, not wanting to reveal my limited computer skills. Penny knew already, but I was certain Alice would think there was some psychological implication to my inability to keep up with the times.

"Have you found any pictures?" Alice asked again.

"A few," I said. "I don't remember which links showed me them, though. Oh, wait, this was one."

I clicked on it and was taken to the website for the *New York Times*. I had seen a picture here of a performance that had earned an entire article in the Entertainment section.

"Will you look at that," Alice murmured. "She really is famous."

"I don't know about *she*..." I muttered in return.

Once the image had fully loaded, which only took about five minutes, we could see clearly the star of the show: Casper. And a bit of Maya's elbow.

"He's even posing!" said Penny.

"I saw a macaw once at an aquarium that posed whenever the camera came out," I said, recalling my visit to the National Aquarium in Baltimore.

"You saw a bird at an aquarium?" Penny asked, making a face at Henny like she thought I was joking.

"Yes," I said. "They had everything from sloths to kookaburras."

"Ooo, I've always wanted to see a kookaburra," said Penny. She never would, unfortunately, unless one happened to move onto our land someday. Penny had never left Paca Springs, and her severe anxiety would probably never allow her to leave. Even with Henny's help.

I clicked out of the link and back to the search engine results.

"Have you looked at that one yet?" Alice asked, leaning over my shoulder to point at a link at the top of the page.

"Yes, this is the Casper the Whistling Cockatiel website," I said, clicking the link again so they could see it.

Naturally, it had been the first site to come up, and I'd collected what information I could from it. The background story of how Maya and Casper had found each other I'd already heard from Maya herself: how she'd saved him and in return he'd saved her when she lost her voice.

"There's not a lot of pictures of Maya," Alice pointed out, pushing up her glasses. "Lots of Casper performing, but only a few including Maya."

"She doesn't look very happy in any of them, either," I realized. "The way she talked about the joy Casper brought her, I would have thought she'd be smiling in more photos. She looks like she's forcing herself to have a good time."

Alice sniffed. "Just another fact in support of my theory that Maya was rather jealous of her show business partner."

"I wonder how long it took her to train Casper," Penny said, eyeing Henny like she was wondering if she could do the same.

"I saw a chicken on a show once that could play the piano," I said with a chuckle.

"*Golden Girls*," said Alice, her gaze still focused on the computer screen.

"Seventeen years," a quiet voice said behind us and we all whirled around.

Maya stood in the doorway, her hair hanging limply about her drawn face, dark circles under her eyes.

"Seventeen years I had Casper," she said. "And all that time I was still training him."

"Wow," said Penny, her admiration evident in her voice.

"I hope you don't mind," Maya said. "I heard voices saying Casper's name and wanted to see who it was."

"Of course we don't mind. We were just trying to learn more about your career, since we haven't known you two very long and we weren't sure you wanted to talk about him," said Penny, explaining swiftly what I couldn't get my mouth to say.

Maya sighed. "You're right. I don't really want to talk about him yet."

"Have you thought any more about a memorial tour?" I asked. "Looks like Casper had more fans than I could've ever imagined for a whistling cockatiel." I waved toward the computer screen filled with photos.

Maya smiled at the sight. "He sure did love his fans."

"I guess that makes this fate," yet another new voice said from behind Maya as Beatrice joined us, as well.

Soon we'd have all eight members of the OBS in one tiny office. Plus Henny.

It was like a real-life clown car. Or a bad joke.

"Now, I know you don't want to see me," Beatrice began, one hand raised in supplication, "but I've come in good faith on behalf of the entire production of *Wizard of Oz*. I heard you're able to whistle, so we'd like to invite you to join Dorothy in a whistling duet during the song, 'Somewhere Over the Rainbow!'"

My eyes widened, as did Maya's. "What a wonderful idea!" I said enthusiastically.

"I figured it might've been something Casper had done professionally during his long career, and I wanted to make it up to you for whatever tensions and misunderstandings there've been between us lately," said Beatrice with one of her heartwarming smiles.

And then she pulled out a stuffed cockatiel. "We even have a cockatiel for you."

Maya's hand flew to her mouth in shock, as did most everyone's in the room.

"Wait, wait!" Beatrice cried, her face stricken. "It's not real. We just thought you'd like something to stand in memoriam of Casper. It's just a prop from the storage closet." She banged the floppy cockatiel against the doorframe as if to show the truth.

It was the wrong move.

"I cannot believe you, Beatrice. I just cannot—" Maya couldn't finish. She ran out of the room.

"And you started so well," Alice murmured with a shake of her head.

{ 18 }

In Which We Recall Lamb Chop

"I thought she'd be pleased as punch!" said Beatrice sadly, shaking her head at the fake cockatiel. "I guess this was one step too far?"

I bit my lip. Yeah, in my opinion, it was about ten steps too far, with a leap thrown in for good measure. I wasn't sure what to say to Beatrice. She looked absolutely miserable.

"I blew it, didn't I?" she said, and I realized she was about to start crying.

"It's all right, honey," Penny said, wrapping her free arm around Beatrice's shoulders and giving her a squeeze.

"It's always difficult to know exactly what is best to do for someone who is in the midst of grief," Alice said, pushing her glasses up her nose.

"Perhaps we best get rid of this," I said, taking the cockatiel. "I'll see if one of Jules's kids want it."

"Good idea," said Penny.

Slings and Sparrows

I left the other two with Beatrice and found Jackie in the kitchen. I was surprised she'd been able to get Aunt Connie out of the café on a Sunday, but when she pointed me toward the park, I knew it was because of Auntie's one weakness: her great-grandkids.

I found them easily enough—just had to follow the screams of laughter—and joined Aunt Connie beside a bench near where Chris and Nicole were racing and chasing all over a wooden jungle gym. Naturally, one would think she'd be seated on the bench. But not Auntie. She was dancing a jig next to it, and it wasn't because she needed to use the restroom.

I sometimes wondered if Auntie could hear music the rest of us could not.

"When I was a kid, we had to play in the crick," I said as I joined the eighty-five-year-old. "I knew even then I was lucky I had a crick to play in, and no mother to tell me not to get my stockings dirty."

Aunt Connie laughed, shaking her head in rhythm to her steps. "I remember those stocking fiascos. Nurse would terrorize me so!"

I laughed with her. You just couldn't help joining in when Auntie laughed. She was infectious. If everyone had an Aunt Connie in their life, the world would be a happier place.

"My how things have changed," I murmured, watching the kids slide down what was sure to be a burning hot metal slide.

"And yet, not at all," Auntie replied.

"The internet? Computers? Cellular phones? Surely the fast-paced technology of today strikes fear into your heart for the future, having grown up in what? The 1920s?"

Auntie smiled. "Yes, born in 1912 and now about to welcome in a new century. You'd think times have changed, but they really haven't. There is nothing new under the sun."

I cocked my head at her.

"Yes, I remember a time when my mother was a suffragette, fighting for women's rights, and now we've got women officers in the military. I remember my neighbor in Boston, Dr. Anne Caroline Cox, who was one of the first female doctors. She inspired me to follow my passions and become the woman I am today. So yes, things have changed. But the general idea of people themselves? People haven't changed in the slightest."

This topic was one of the few that showed Aunt Connie's more solemn side. I'd heard some of this before, and it was most likely because of hearing this over and over again that I'd taken an interest in history and made my focus the Victorian era, the time period just before my parents' generation.

"Governments still rise and fall. The economy still shifts and breaks. Marriages still struggle to find that balance of equality. Parents still live in fear of the world their children will inherit. And children will always find time to play with stuffed animals." She pointed to the cockatiel in my hand. "Juliette told me you were researching on the internet. Doing some hands-on research, too?"

"Actually, this needs to stay as far away from Maya as possible. I thought Nicole and Chris might like it."

"That's very thoughtful," said Auntie with a smile, taking the cockatiel out of my palm. "I'll give it to them later. It wouldn't last long on the playground." She flipped the bird around and looked into its little glass eyes. "Nicole's favorite stuffed animal right now is a puppet from a TV show."

"Which show is popular now?"

"*Wishbone* is Jules's favorite, but I think it might go over the children's heads a little at this age. It's about a dog who acts out literature. You'd love it. It's on PBS."

"I think I may have actually caught an episode or two before. A little Jack Russell? Playing Romeo or Tom Sawyer or Sherlock? I'm pretty sure my grandkids watch it. I think it's a fantastic idea. It's sure to get kids excited about literature."

"Precisely. I hope it's still on as Chris and Nicole get older. Right now they're all about *Sesame Street* and *Lamb Chop*."

I laughed at her. "Like with mint jelly?"

"No." Aunt Connie waved her hand. "And lamb is much better in curry—I'll make it for you sometime."

The only time I ever ate meat was with Aunt Connie, who was almost impossible to turn down when it came to at least trying her food. I had to admit, once it was smothered and cooked in her seasonings, I might have even eaten chicken.

"*Lamb Chop* is another TV show. Let's see, I think it's Lamb Chop, Charlie Horse, and Hush Puppy?"

I shook my head and gave Auntie my special look for crazy people.

"'The Song That Never Ends'?"

"Oh my goodness!" I cried, my eyes widening with recognition now. "Yes! The ventriloquist show. That lady with the curly hair." I pointed to Aunt Connie's coiffure.

"Shari Lewis," Auntie said with a nod and a tap from foot to foot.

"I'm afraid it's another show I've only caught in passing with the grandkids. Penny and I are more often watching things like *Frasier* and *Everybody Loves Raymond*."

Auntie looked out at the kids. "Chris and Nicole have all the puppets. They lost the first Charlie Horse at a playground and I had to buy a second one because he was Chris's favorite." She waved the cockatiel in her hand. "So that's why I'll be keeping this bird off the playground."

"Ah, I see. Now I get the connected thought."

Aunt Connie laughed again. "You're lucky you had only the one kid. They turn all your thoughts into spaghetti." She tapped her curly white head. "Everything is connected but you can't remember why."

"You know," I said, another connection flying through my brain, "I once saw a production of *Wizard of Oz* where the Wizard performed with a dummy."

Aunt Connie raised her brows at me, giving me her version of the crazy lady look.

"Ventriloquism," I said. "Shari Lewis, ventriloquism, that stuffed cockatiel came from Beatrice, who's working on *Wizard of Oz*..." I held out my palm.

"Ah," said Auntie, "that was what I was missing. So, how did the Wizard use the dummy?"

"It replaced the big face that the Wizard speaks through."

Auntie's eyes widened. "Are they doing it that way here?"

"Oh no!" I said, waving my hands. "This one's *steampunk*."

"What is 'steampunk?'" Aunt Connie asked.

"I don't think anyone is really sure," I said with a shrug. "We'll just have to see the production to find out."

Slings and Sparrows

Auntie laughed and did a double tap step. "I guess so."

She returned her focus to the kids.

"Thanks, by the way," I said.

"For what?"

"Now I'm gonna have 'The Song That Never Ends' stuck in my head for the rest of the day…"

{ 19 }

In Which Maya is Reborn

The Stuffed Bird Catastrophe, as it came to be known, did not help matters between Maya and Beatrice. Beatrice kept herself busy with all the necessary last-minute costuming needs, and avoided coming by our house for tea and Mahjong like she usually did every Monday afternoon. But somewhere along the way they must've crossed paths again, because that night, Maya marched into the dining room and announced to Penny and me that she was leaving.

"I can't stay here another minute. I won't continue to live so near that...*woman*. I have to get out of here."

"That might not be a bad idea," I said. "I've always found getting away for a little while a good way to clear my head. You could drive up to Vermont—it's lovely this time of year—or Boston or New York City for a change of pace?"

"I didn't mean for a vacation," Maya said, a bit more rudely than she'd probably intended. "Everything here reminds me of

Slings and Sparrows

Casper and my hopes to finally settle down and retire. Instead, I've lost Casper and no one seems to care!" she choked.

"We care!" Penny and I both said in chorus.

"We'd help you if we only knew how," Penny said, reaching out to take Maya's hand.

"And if you'd let us," I said.

Maya sniffed. "There's nothing you can do but get me moving boxes. I'm moving out next weekend."

There wasn't much for her to move out, considering that all her things were still in storage while we waited for her house to be finished. But I understood she was making more of an emotional statement than a realistic one.

"Really? It's that bad?" I asked.

Maya nodded and avoided our eyes.

"I'm so sorry, Maya," Penny said quietly. "I wish we could do more."

Maya's face softened and she took a steadying breath. "It's all right, Penny. It's not your fault, or yours," she said to me. "I just... I need to move forward. I've already got my first performance booked for myself in Pittsburgh two weeks from now."

"You're going to perform?" I asked.

Maya nodded. "It was your idea, Goose. Like you suggested, I'll be whistling in Casper's memory."

"That's wonderful," cried Penny, tears of joy springing to her eyes. She was such an empathetic person.

"Thank you," said Maya, wiping the back of her hand across her wet eyes. "I'm sorry it has to be this way."

"Do you want your down payment back?" I asked, ever the realist. We'd needed to build a new house on our land for the next OBS member anyway, and when Maya turned up, she'd offered to give us a down payment toward the house against the first six months of her rent. The foundation for Maya's house had been poured, so we'd already spent the money she'd given us. I hoped she didn't want it back.

"Keep it. Pay it forward. Maybe it'll help the next poor soul who finds herself here," Maya said. Then she swept out of the room before we could say another word.

Penny and I exchanged glances.

"Well, I guess that's that," I said.

"What a terrible way to go." Penny shook her head.

"It's not like she's dying. If anything, she's reborn, beginning a new life."

Penny looked at Henny and rubbed her hand over her feathers. "I don't know what I'd do if you were murdered."

"Don't think like that," I said.

Penny frowned at me. "You're saying if someone shot Tomi or Tuppence you wouldn't be outraged, spending all your time tracking down the killer?"

"Of course I would. But Maya already thinks she knows the killer: Beatrice."

Penny shook her head. "I think deep down Maya knows Beatrice didn't do it. She just desperately wants it to be Beatrice because that gets someone out of her life she doesn't like for other reasons."

"Well, it doesn't matter anymore," I said, standing up. "Maya won't have to deal with Beatrice anymore. She's moving out."

Penny sighed. "Yes, but I still want to know who did it."

So did I.

Slings and Sparrows

Penny's mention of Tomi and Tuppence made me realize I hadn't seen my geese in a couple of days. Even though there was no gander, sometimes they got it into their heads that they needed to brood and sit on their eggs in the hopes of making them hatch, especially if I was distracted and hadn't had time to collect their eggs. They found the craziest places to hide: amongst the reeds and cattails around the pond, or behind the freezers and canning shelves in the basement. For being such tall geese, standing at a little over three feet when their posture was perfect, they could tuck into the most amazing places.

I decided to take a little evening walk to their usual haunts, to see if I could find them.

Now, I didn't normally let things worry me. I tended to shrug things off like water off a duck's—or goose's—back. But when I couldn't find them, I admit, my heart sped up a little. I refused to let it get to me even then, though. After all, they could take care of themselves. So I went to bed, telling myself I'd wake up and there they'd be, honking at the peacock to stop yelping at the sunrise.

But the next morning they still weren't there.

"You look worried, Goose," Penny said at breakfast, forever reading my thoughts whether I wanted her to or not.

"It's nothing," I said with a wave of my hand, trying to focus on my jam and toast.

"Are you worried about Maya moving out? I'm sure we'll find someone new soon enough. Especially since her house is halfway done already."

"No, it's not that. I can't believe she left us the down payment, though. She must be more financially stable than we'd realized."

Penny nodded. "Then what is it? What's worrying you? Please, tell me. I have enough on my mind with Casper's death, I don't need to be worried about you, too."

I sighed. "It's just that—" I paused.

I really didn't want to burden her, but she'd just keep asking till I gave it up.

Finally I muttered, "I haven't seen Tomi and Tuppence since Saturday when you and I walked back from the museum together."

Penny set down her orange juice, her eyes wide, her hand stilling on Henny's back. Henny also looked at me with concern, her head cocked as she eyed me carefully.

"I'm sure it's nothing. They're probably around here somewhere. They can't have gone far," all the platitudes spilling out that I'd told myself repeatedly since last night.

I couldn't believe I'd not noticed their disappearance for over forty-eight hours. I'd refilled their food bowls and switched out their waters just like I did every day, twice a day, but I'd been so lost in my own thoughts I hadn't noticed if they'd actually touched their food or water. It *was* odd that I didn't see them to say "honk" to at some point during the day.

"Goose, what if—" Penny stopped herself, an absolutely horrified look on her face.

"What if...what?"

Slings and Sparrows

    Penny looked at Henny, then back at me, then over her shoulder toward the doorway leading into the rest of the house, then back at me.

    "Penny, spit it out," I said, my nerves getting to me.

    "What if…something…happened…" Penny looked down at Henny again. "Like what happened to Casper?"

{ 20 }

In Which Tomi and Tuppence Go Missing

My heart stopped. I swear it literally did.

It was one thing to think a thing, but to hear my greatest fear voiced by Penny...

My sister reached across the table and squeezed my hand. "Goose, I didn't mean to...I mean, I may be wrong. They could be just fine."

I stood up. "I'm going to go find them."

I didn't say "search for them" or "look for them," I said "find them" on purpose, because I was going to *find* them. There was no other choice.

I began by marching upstairs and knocking on Maya's door. It took a couple moments, but she finally did open her door to me, wrapped in a silk robe, her bronze hair a tangled mess, her eyes gluey with sleep.

"Goose?" she said, but then her face cleared and she looked concerned. "Goose, what is it? Don't tell me you found—"

"No, I'm sorry, Maya. I don't have news about Casper, but I was wondering if you'd seen Tomi and Tuppence?"

"Tomi and Tuppence? Your geese?" The way she said it was like she'd never met them before, or that it had never occurred to her that I might care about them as much as she cared about her stupid songbird. And after they'd grieved with her and everything.

"Yes, my geese. Have you seen them at all this weekend?"

Maya shook her head slowly. "No, I'm afraid I haven't. But then, I've been a bit distracted."

Yes, we'd all been distracted. Distracted by the death of a cockatiel that half the world cared about, so why would anyone care about two geese that only mattered to one silly old woman?

"Thanks," I muttered, and fled down the stairs and out the door.

I began to make the rounds of the property. They'd never gone too far before, and I knew if they wandered as far as town, someone was bound to call it in.

Penny caught up to me and offered to stop by the police station on the way to the museum, but it made me blush to think of bothering those nice men and women with missing birds when they no doubt had bigger matters on their hands: graffitied parks and stolen stop signs and the like. So, instead, she said she'd pop in at the Quaint Quail to see if anyone had seen or heard two geese cruising through town.

By the time I reached Sable's, I was less worried about sounding insane. As she opened her door, I asked if Hugin could track like a falcon.

Sable shook her head. "I don't think so. At least, I've never heard of a raven doing that, though they are very intelligent. You could probably teach a raven almost anything if given the time."

"Too bad," I said. I heard a rustling sound to my left and turned expectantly, but it was only a small rabbit skittering away from Hugin as he came out to preen in the sun.

"So let me get this straight: you're on a wild goose chase?" Sable smiled.

I might have smiled, too, if I hadn't been so worried.

Sable seemed to notice and offered to walk about with me and look for Tomi and Tuppence.

"Are you sure? Don't you have to teach?" I asked, but I was grateful for the offer. I was really trying not to let the image of Casper held in Maya's hands get to me, but it had wiggled into my brain the way those geese had wiggled into my heart, and wouldn't let go.

"Not on Tuesdays." Sable closed the door behind her before turning to suggest, "Have you checked the pond?"

I tried to tell her kindly that of course I had, but it came out a bit gruffer than I'd intended. Sweet Sable just ignored my tone, taking it in stride as always.

"Let's check it one more time. Two pairs of eyes are better than one."

"Better than one, better than one," Hugin crowed.

"Maybe three pairs," Sable said, and sure enough, Hugin followed us back to the pond.

We circled it slowly, shoving the high reeds to the side but being careful with every step. Each moment I half expected to part the cattails to find Tomi or Tuppence on nests, blinking up at me as if to say, "What were you worried about? We've been here all along."

But they weren't.

"Nothing," I grunted as we completed our rounds.

Sable shook her head. "Not here, either. Though I did find Casper's gravesite."

"Really?" I tried to be interested, but for now I was more concerned about my geese, and whether they'd be joining Casper.

"Yeah, in the holler to the north, near the crick that feeds into the pond. Looks like Maya had Joseph carve her a marker and everything."

Guess that explained what she wanted to speak with him about the other day.

"Mmhm," I murmured.

"All right," Sable said, noticing my distracted state. "Where do you want to try next?"

"Everywhere," I said crazily.

So we did. At Beatrice's, she paused her work long enough to wave for us to have a look around, but she hadn't seen them. I knew if they were anywhere near the peacocks, we'd hear the noise, as the two types of birds liked to yelp and honk at one another in playful, or perhaps not-so-playful banter.

We tried Alice's next, but again, I strongly doubted they'd be there, given their extreme dislike for the guinea fowl and their ratcheting squeaky-gate noises, which were constant if they felt their space was being violated. At least a goose only honked when he had something to tell you.

"If I were a goose, I'd feel right at home amongst ducks, wouldn't you?" Sable suggested, as we headed toward Ruth's.

I certainly thought Tomi and Tuppence would prefer the ducks' company to the guinea fowl or peacocks, so I let Sable lead the way.

The ducks were out in the ponds next to Ruth's house, a simple stone cottage that wouldn't have looked out of place if you'd happened across it in the wilds of northern Wales. The remains of the cottage had been standing on the property long enough that our dad and his brother, not to mention Penny and I, had used it as a playhouse. With Ruth's arrival, we'd taken the opportunity, and her generous down payment, to turn it into someplace livable.

A low stone wall ran down either side of her property to the north and south, marking it out from the rest of the acreage and serving as an attempt to keep her ducks closer to her home and her ponds. If they'd discovered there was another, larger pond on the other side of the property, next to Penny and me, they'd no doubt have waddled their little way right over and made themselves at home, and I didn't think Tomi and Tuppence would have appreciated that.

As we approached, the ducks were happily splashing and dunking under the water, quacking and laughing and having quite the raucous pool party.

My heart sank at the lack of two large white geese amongst them.

"They're not here," I said, trying to think positively but failing miserably.

"Let's go knock on the door, at least," Sable said, marching up to Ruth's front door and knocking solidly.

"Who is it?" I heard Ruth call from inside.

Sable replied and Ruth opened the door. "Hello! How's the weather out there? My old war wound has been telling me to expect rain." She gave her leg a pat—I *told* you it would come up—and leaned on her cane. "Oh, dear, or maybe something worse?" Her gaze focused on our faces.

"We're on the hunt for a couple of wandering geese," Sable said. "Tomi and Tuppence—have you happened upon them?"

Ruth shook her head. "No, I'm afraid not. I'd know immediately if they were out in the ponds with the ducks. They raise the most frightful ruckus, which is why I've *encouraged* them to keep out when they've come this way."

"When's the last time you saw them?" I asked.

Ruth looked toward the sky, as though the sun were her clock. "A few days."

I brightened. "Saturday, maybe?"

Ruth considered again. "Yes, I suppose so."

"What were they doing?"

"Following at Maya's heels, as usual," Ruth said.

"Usual? They've never seemed to like her especially before."

Ruth smiled slightly. "It seems that since Casper's demise, they've taken to following Maya about wherever she goes."

"Perhaps in an attempt to brighten her spirits," Sable suggested.

I liked that idea, and it sounded like something they'd do after seeing their empathetic grief for Maya on that first day.

"Have you seen them following her since Saturday?"

"No, I suppose not," Ruth admitted. "Odd. Come to think of it, the last I saw them was when we…"

I raised my eyebrow at Ruth's hesitation. But then—

"I heard it, too," said Sable.

Ruth stepped out onto her porch, leading with her cane, as Sable and I walked slowly down into the front yard and stood very still, our ears perked like a couple of rabbits.

"Honk!"

"Honk, honk!"

{ 21 }

In Which We Discover Freezers

A wave of relief swept over me from head to foot as I ran pell-mell toward the sound.

"Honk!"

"Honk, honk!"

The honking was muffled, and it was a wonder we'd heard it at all over the squabbling of the ducks in the ponds. They'd quieted just long enough for me to hear it.

"Where *are* they?" I cried in irritation, as we rounded the house and still there was no sign of them.

I heard Ruth's muck boots slapping the muddy ground behind us as she took her time joining us, and we all strained our ears again.

This time, when we heard the honking, Ruth's face went white.

"Oh, dear," she muttered.

"What is it?" I asked, wondering if my warm feeling of relief had come too soon.

"I know where they are," she said.

She led the way back to the edge of her property line, where an old shed stood with gardening supplies spilling out of buckets under cracked windows and stacked alongside crumbling slate stone walls.

From within I heard the distinct sound of two rather distressed geese.

"How in the blue blazes did they get in there?" I asked.

Ruth shook her head. She hobbled to the old door and jiggled the handle, muttering as she did so. "I knew I'd locked this... So how did... I'll be right back."

"What—?" I watched as Ruth slowly limped back to the house. "Where is she going?" I asked Sable, who shrugged in response.

"Don't worry, girls, we'll get you out in a minute!" I called, pressing my face to one of the dirty windows in an attempt to see inside.

I had to let my eyes adjust to the darkness within, but when they did, I could just make out two enormous freezers and stacks of crates and boxes and other gardening equipment.

One crate was open, revealing a large, still pile of feathers.

"Oh my— Tomi! Tuppence!" I cried in anguish.

"Goose?" Sable asked in concern, coming up beside me and putting a hand on my shoulder to see what had caused my cry.

She peered inside, then pulled me away from the window.

"It's not them, Goose. Listen to me: it's not them." She had to practically shake me to get me to hear her. "Listen! They're honking! They wouldn't be honking if that pile of feathers was theirs!"

I was able to finally clear my mind long enough to hear their honks of distress again, and once I did, I took a deep breath, having apparently stopped breathing for a minute.

"Ha," I half breathed, half laughed in relief. "You're right. Of course, you're right."

"They probably snuck into the shed to find a nice, quiet place to brood. I bet that pile of feathers is a nest."

I nodded dumbly again.

"Let's have a look around and see if we can figure out how they got in," Sable suggested, taking me by the arm before I could argue.

We made a circuit around the shed, discovering we could only access three sides, as one side was pressed right up against the slate wall. Although the wood was rather old, there were no holes large enough for a goose to push through, even though I knew they could sometimes squeeze into spaces barely large enough to accommodate a duck.

"I don't get it," Sable said, shaking her head as we came back around to the door. "No cracks, no leaks, no broken windows. I'm at a loss as to how they got inside."

"It's a regular locked room mystery," I muttered.

"At least we know where they are now," Sable said, patting my shoulder. "Don't worry, we'll have them out in a jiffy."

In answer, we heard Ruth approaching us once again, still moving without the haste the situation required, in my opinion. "Here I come!" she called.

Under her free arm, she carried a stuffed duck.

Before I could ask what the duck was for, she reached *inside* it and pulled out an old rusted key.

My jaw dropped. The duck was a regular Maltese Falcon!

Ruth inserted the key and turned the handle, and this time the door opened inward with a juddering thud.

In a whirlwind of white feathers, orange feet, and orange beaks, my two beautiful geese flew out and practically into my arms.

They didn't seem overly pleased to see any of us, not even me, and quickly waddle-flew off toward the ducks, eager to make up for lost time.

"You think the ducks did it?" Sable asked with a grin.

I was not in the mood, and Ruth still looked gray about the gills.

"*What* is in that shed?" I asked, pushing past her as she tried to pull the door to and lock it again.

I had to let my eyes adjust to the poor lighting, but once they did, I could see once more the pile of feathers tucked back amongst the stacks of boxes between the two freezers. Each one was probably twenty-four cubic feet, about the size of the one Penny and I used for storing the vegetables and fruits we didn't get around to canning at the end of summer.

"They just look like freezers," Sable said, who'd followed me in.

"They *are* just freezers," said Ruth, irritably.

"That's not what concerns me," I said. "What is that pile of feathers? What is going on in here?"

Ruth crossed the room and closed the lid on the crate that held the feathers, as if by hiding them from view she could negate my seeing them and asking about them.

"Nothing. Absolutely nothing," Ruth said, crossing her arms and avoiding my eyes.

I exchanged glances with Sable.

"Then why were you so upset to learn the geese were in here?" I asked, searching her face.

Ruth continued avoiding my eyes, staring at the freezers. "I...collect the feathers and sprinkle them about the yard in case the ducks want to use them for their nests."

I exchanged another glance with Sable.

"Seems like an awful lot of trouble to go to," I said. "Don't the ducks use their feathers naturally? Without your assistance?"

"Ye-es," Ruth admitted hesitantly, drawing out the word.

What was in those freezers? It clearly wasn't fruits and veggies. My heart thumped like Edgar Allan Poe's Tell-Tale Heart, and I couldn't help but wonder if I opened one would I find a...body?

Ruth sighed. "Fine, I'll tell you, because it would be worse if you opened them and found out."

{ 22 }

In Which We Learn What's In the Freezers

"I've been butchering and selling my ducks and their feathers for a little extra cash," Ruth said, finally glancing up at me and down again. "I didn't want to tell you because, well…look at your reaction to my mention of Joseph the other day…and my stuffed ducks and, well…I figured it best if you didn't know."

I wasn't wrong. It was a body. Or bodies.

Ruth's accent slipped away from British back to her American roots as she fluttered on. "Social security ain't what it used to be and sure I've got some money put by and don't worry I can continue to pay my rent but…"

I blew out. "No, I don't like it, but I especially don't like that you lied to me about it and kept it from me." I put my hands on my hips.

Ruth grimaced and made a face.

"What?" I asked.

"Well… If you'd ever once come over to my house and visited, you'd have seen I have a lovely collection. I like to get my favorite ducks stuffed. They're really quite delightful company…"

"Like that poor fellow?" I asked, pointing to the duck she still had tucked under her arm. "I can't believe you hid a key inside him."

Sable snorted. "I think it's downright genius, myself. Who'd ever think of searching for a key up a duck's butt?"

When she put it that way, I supposed it was rather funny.

"Joseph do that for you?" Sable asked.

Ruth nodded, but still wouldn't look at me.

"Is this where you store those ducks?" I asked, waving toward the freezers. "Before taking them to Joseph downtown?"

"Well, not Joseph. He only takes the ones I want stuffed. I sell the butchered ones to—"

I held up a hand to stop her. "I don't want to know." I sighed and let my hands fall to my sides. "Okay, anything else you need to admit to me?"

Ruth shook her head. "No."

"You sure? Nothing concerning the catching and locking up of my geese? Perhaps with the intent to butcher or stuff them?"

"No!" Ruth cried, taking a step back, her eyes wide. "No, I'd never! I swear, I don't know how they got in here! I mean—" She looked about the dark room and made a face. "I mean, I might know how, and I feel absolutely gutted about it, but it's possible—however unlikely—that they might have maybe…" She muttered something to the duck in her arm. I had to ask her to repeat herself.

"They may have followed Maya in here and then *accidentally* gotten locked in when we left," she repeated, only slightly more clearly than previously.

"I see," I said softly, trying to temper my anger.

"Now, Goose, you can see how sorry she is," Sable said, attempting to mollify me. "It was an accident."

"Awful lot of accidents happening around here lately," I grumbled. "What were you two doing in here? Maya buried Casper, she didn't have him stuffed." I glanced at the stuffed duck. "Unless she *also* lied to me and dug a false grave just to keep me off the scent."

Ruth was shaking her head. "No, that was why she came to me. She needed a box."

"A box?" I repeated.

"A coffin, you know, to bury him in."

"Why didn't she just use a shoebox?" Sable asked.

I was thankful Penny wasn't nearby. She'd never buried a Henny in a shoebox. She preferred wooden boxes that she could engrave with a wood-burner with pretty decorations and such. Sometimes they turned out too pretty to bury, in my opinion, but that didn't stop her. She said it was for Henny, not for us. Like how the pharaohs buried themselves with gold and jewels.

"She wanted something special," Ruth said, moving toward a stack of boxes in a corner. She grabbed one and brought it over to us. "She took one of these."

The box was made of styrofoam. Nothing fancy.

"Not very glamorous for a famous songbird," Sable said, following my thoughts.

I wondered if Penny should have offered her skills at woodburning so Maya didn't have to settle for something like this.

"She said she was going to bedazzle it or something," Ruth said. "She came to me asking about taxidermy, and I pointed her to Joseph, but then the more we talked, the more she seemed disinclined toward the idea, and preferred to bury him instead."

Smart woman, I thought.

"So I offered to find her a box that would preserve him a little longer, should she change her mind over the next few days," Ruth continued.

"I have a feeling that styrofoam is gonna be around a lot longer than he is," Sable said, and I agreed. I'd stopped using the stuff after hearing it took something like five hundred years to decompose.

I strongly doubted Maya would be digging up her bird again. She'd probably just taken the box to get Ruth to stop pestering her about stuffing him and turning him into a hideyhole for her keys.

I shivered and drifted back out into the sunlight.

The gloominess of the little shed was getting to me, and poor Tomi and Tuppence had been trapped in here for over two days.

And I hadn't noticed.

That was the worst part of it all. The guilt I felt at not noticing my own birds had disappeared. I didn't even like Casper. Who cared who killed him? Who cared if it was Beatrice or Joseph or...

"Are you sure the geese followed you and Maya here and just got locked inside by accident?" I asked, as Ruth and Sable joined me.

"That must be what happened," Ruth said sheepishly. "I haven't seen them since then, and Maya and I were busy talking about Casper, and could very easily have not noticed they were left behind."

"What are you thinking, Goose?" Sable asked quizzically.

"I was just thinking. It's also possible someone else herded them in here and locked them up, so as to distract me."

"Distract you from what?" Ruth asked.

"Distract me from Casper's murder." I glanced at the stuffed duck in Ruth's arm. "Penny and I have kind of taken it upon ourselves to figure out whodunnit. I was distracted enough to not notice Tomi and Tuppence were missing, and now I've been distracted enough looking for them to stop questioning people about Casper's murder."

"No one would lock up your geese on purpose," Sable said with a derisive chuckle.

"Does Joseph know about this shed?" I asked, turning to Ruth.

"Yes," Ruth said slowly, leaning heavily on her cane. "I've sometimes had him come out to get the duck himself, depending on his availability and my schedule."

"So he knew where to find the key?"

Ruth nodded. "He's the only other person who does."

Sable touched my elbow. "Now, Goose, you can't really be thinking—"

"Joseph knew," I said, pulling my arm from her. "And he does taxidermy and Casper was pinned with taxidermy pins. And he's in the very middle of the love triangle between Beatrice and Maya."

"You said Beatrice—"

"I know he's involved somehow," I said, pushing past the other two and away from the dratted shed.

Time to once more visit the hardware store.

{ 23 }

In Which I Don't Exactly Act My Age

"Joseph Hollister, what, may I ask, do you have against geese?" I yelled, throwing myself through the front door of the hardware store.

"What?" he responded, a master of repartee.

"Hey, Joseph." A flash of black in my peripheral vision told me Sable had followed me into the store. She'd forcefully "suggested" she give me a ride into town, though she'd been kind enough not to interrupt my rambling on our way over. "She's wondering if you locked up her geese in Ruth's shed with plans to stuff them."

"What?" he said again. Did the old man need a hearing aid?

"You heard her. Answer the lady!" I said, slapping the counter with both hands.

"I have no idea what you're talking about," he said coolly.

I glared.

"Okay, thanks, Joseph." Sable grabbed my arm as though she intended to haul me away from the confrontation by force.

I was only three years older than her and I had a good foot on her, so there was no way I was giving up the fight on behalf of my geese.

"I know you had something to do with it. Only you could have known where to find the key!"

A bell tinkled behind me and I whirled on the newcomer, only to find Maya once again interrupting my interrogation of Joseph.

"Goose!" she said in surprise. Her eyes took in the looks on each of our faces and her brow furrowed. "What's going on here?"

Before I could answer, Sable filled her in.

"But I don't understand why you think Joseph did it?" Maya said. "I was just out there with Ruth and—"

"The key—"

"My gosh, you're like a retriever with that thing. Let it go, Goose," Sable said firmly.

I growled and crossed my arms, fully aware of how petulant I was being. I just wanted someone to pay for this atrocity against goose-dom. Killing cockatiels was one thing, but when they came after my own—now it was personal.

"Joseph didn't do it," said Maya, coming to stand before me at his counter.

"How do you know?" I asked, looking from her to Joseph, who looked just as mystified.

"I just do. Now, I think it's time the two of you left."

My jaw almost dropped at her impertinence. Sable swooped in and took advantage of my momentary shock, swiftly manhandling me out the door.

On the sidewalk, she turned me to face her.

"Wow, Goose, I know you care about your geese, but good grief. There's no need to fly into a rage. I know you're menopausal but jiminy... You're acting worse than Maya did about Casper—and Casper died! At least Tomi and Tuppence are okay!"

The door to the hardware store swung open and Joseph joined us.

He was holding a white handkerchief like it was a flag of surrender. If I hadn't been so blinking mad at him I might've smiled.

"I'm sorry someone did that to you, Goose," he said, coming up to us. "I mean, to your geese. I'm sure it must've scared you to find them locked up like that, especially in a place Ruth always warned me never to talk to you about—which I told her wasn't a problem as I didn't know you. But now I do, and I'm sorry," he finished.

Then he nodded and made his way back up the steps into his store.

"Joseph," I called.

He turned.

"Thank you," I said.

He nodded and rang the bell above his own shop door as he entered.

"That was awfully nice of him." Sable gave my shoulder a nudge, as if Joseph had just asked me to the high school prom.

Slings and Sparrows

I gave her a look. "I still want to know who did it. And why."

"I think Ruth gave you a perfectly reasonable explanation for it. Why are you so convinced someone did it on purpose? Do you think it has something to do with Casper's death?"

I nodded slowly. "It must." Why didn't she see it? "Am I getting too close to the truth? I don't feel like I've learned anything important. And if there's a serial bird murderer out there, why only lock up Tomi and Tuppence? Why not—you know..."

"Yeah, I know," Sable said, patting my shoulder gently. "But contrary to what you may think, you're not in the middle of a *Thin Man* movie. I think you should take the rest of the day off. Even the best detective takes a break. Relax, put your feet up, spend some time watching Tomi and Tuppence. You know, just to reaffirm to yourself that they're okay now."

I pictured myself sitting and reading some Agatha Christie to Tomi and Tuppence, or possibly something older like an Anna Katharine Green mystery, while they paddled happily in the pond. "I sure like the sound of that."

"Tomorrow you can resume detective work. I've got the perfect setup for you: Beatrice has asked me to swing by in the afternoon to model some of the costumes she's finishing up for the show. It's sure to be an entertaining mood-lifter. You could tag along and question her more. The Three Musketeers back together again."

"You're just afraid if you're left alone with Beatrice she'll try to make you wear a dress." I smirked.

"Right in one, detective," Sable said with a smile.

"The worst she could do is try to draft you to be an extra in the play."

Sable grimaced. "That's almost as bad. I've never been one for theater."

"Really? I distinctly recall you delivering a shivering Gothic rendition of Poe's 'Annabel Lee' at an open mic once. I believe you were even dressed in an era-appropriate mourning gown."

Sable gave me a look. "First and last time. And the gown was no doubt Beatrice's doing."

"You never did theater with Joseph or his sister back in Chambersburg?"

Sable shook her head. "Stage fright. I hate getting up in front of people. I've always been more of the bookish nerd gardening type."

"Same here, sister," I said.

Sable raised a brow at me. "Don't you buy your canning vegetables and fruit from me every year because you claim you don't have a green thumb?"

"Alright, so maybe I'm not the bookish nerd *gardening* type, but the first part is accurate." My mind turned back to the couple inside the hardware store. "So, do you think Maya has a chance with Joseph?"

Sable shrugged. "He's a great guy. She'd be lucky to be with him. But I don't think Joseph will ever move away from Chambersburg. If she plans on returning to the limelight, she'll be making a choice between him and her career."

I nodded. "Been there," I said.

Luckily, my husband, Sam, had agreed to pack our collective bags and journey with me around the world, teaching English in countries on almost every continent. It had been this decision that had never left us as sad empty-nesters. Instead,

Slings and Sparrows

we'd counted down the days till Derrick finally moved out for good.

Don't get me wrong: I love my kid. He ended up studying abroad and coming to visit us when we lived in Budapest. How many kids can say that?

"I wonder if that's what she's doing right now," I said, "asking him if he'd go with her?"

But that night, as Maya marched past Penny and me in the living room, I could tell that if she had asked him that question, then she wasn't too pleased with his answer.

{ 24 }

In Which Corsets Are Debated

"Watch where you're sticking, woman!"

"Stop wiggling like a worm and I will, darlin'!"

Sable grunted and then yelped again. "Seriously, Beatrice. Something is sticking into my back! I know I haven't worn a corset since my college days, but I don't think it's supposed to do that!"

Beatrice took a step away from where Sable stood on a stool, and gave her costume a once-over.

I was happily sitting in the corner eating popcorn and watching the two of them reenact Flora and Merryweather arguing over the dress in *Sleeping Beauty*.

Sable had been right: this was both thoroughly entertaining and mood-lifting.

"Let me re-lace it," Beatrice finally admitted.

"Thank you." Sable sighed, proving she wasn't as tightly laced as she'd made out. "Whose crazy outfit is this supposed to be again?"

"The Tin Woman's," said Beatrice, pulling the laces.

Beatrice had done an excellent job suggesting the character in a Victorian style. The long silvery-gray skirt and petticoats, gray long-sleeved lace blouse, and silver-embroidered corset were elegantly simple, and with the added bits of metal Beatrice was attaching all over, along with the funnel hat nearby, it certainly implied the Tin *Woman*.

"And why isn't *she* standing here being tortured?"

"I thought you'd enjoy helping me," said Beatrice, making a face at me as I watched. "If I'd realized you were gonna stand there and whine more than the teenage girl this is meant for, I'd have simply waited for her school day to finish."

Sable rolled her eyes at me but I just smiled and took another handful of popcorn.

"Would it help if I held onto a bedpost or something?" Sable asked, no doubt thinking of that completely inaccurate depiction of corset-wearing from *Gone with the Wind*.

The Victorian lit professor in me just had to set her straight. "Movies like that give corsets a bad name. In reality, corsets were just there to provide structure, to hold things in place."

"And to emphasize all the right curves," Beatrice said with a knowing grin, running a hand down her own figure.

Sable rolled her eyes.

"The myth of the 'sixteen-inch waist' comes from advertisement and propaganda," I continued with my lecture, warming to my theme. "A woman was never able to decrease her waist size with a corset more than a couple inches, so most women were somewhere in the twenty- to thirty-inch range, and even that's proving inaccurate the more photos we uncover through archival research. Women were as varied in size and shape then as they are today."

Beatrice finished re-lacing Sable and filled her mouth with pins as she got back to adjusting the accoutrements.

"Can't you just do this on a model?" Sable complained, fidgeting.

Beatrice raised an eyebrow at Sable as she pinned on more metallic-looking fabric.

"You know what I mean: not a *live* model," Sable clarified.

"The corset doesn't sit right on a dress-form mannequin and I need to see the full effect."

Which sounded bogus to me. It was clear Beatrice was doing this on Sable with a completely ulterior motive. Whether that was to cheer me up or just have a reason to stick pins in our college friend, I wasn't quite sure.

Beatrice pulled the last few pins from her mouth so she could speak clearly. "Besides, the girl wearing this costume always tells me how comfortable she feels in it. Says it gives her an added confidence."

"That's because she's a teenager still struggling with her body image. I'm sixty-two. I left all that behind long ago."

Beatrice and I exchanged a look.

"What?" Sable demanded.

"Do we ever truly leave the playground?" I asked, thinking of my conversation with Aunt Connie the other day.

"We are not so far from those teenage days as we often like to think," Beatrice agreed. "If there's one thing I've learned doing community theater, it's that we all have our insecurities. And they're usually the same ones we hoped we'd outgrow after graduation."

Sable fidgeted again in response. "I'm just saying I don't think fashion is worth it."

This from the Goth who continued to wear all black even in summer heat upwards of ninety degrees.

Beatrice took a step back and crossed her arms. "Are you seriously telling me you're uncomfortable?"

Sable took a deep breath, seemed to realize what she'd just done, and twisted a little from side to side. Finally she shook her head. "Fine, all right. *Now* it's fine."

"See." Beatrice waved to me for support. "It's all about lacing it properly."

"Exactly—the Victorians wore them day and night, no matter their class," I said. "Even maids worked in them."

"Day and *night*?" Sable asked, wide-eyed.

"You'd just loosen the lacing," I said, another handful of popcorn going in. "It was better than taking it off and letting everything...settle, only to have to put it back on in the morning."

"I think there's a point in a woman's age where she should accept that 'settling' is part of nature," said Sable.

She was one to talk. She'd been blessed with a petite frame that meant she could still pass for thirty if she felt like it. Her Goth attire actually helped to make her appear younger, like Morticia Addams—the corset only enhanced the similarity.

I glanced at Beatrice in her Edwardian ensemble, perfectly coiffed and rolled frosted-silver black hair, and carefully made-up face. Meanwhile, here I was, lounging in sweatpants and a T-shirt, shoveling down popcorn like I hadn't a care in the world.

Then again, I was sixty-five, had been happily married all my life, and now with Sam gone, had no interest in a future with a new love interest. As far as I was concerned, I could eat what I wanted, drink what I wanted, and do whatever I wanted for the rest of my life, even if that meant it would end up being shorter than it might have been.

My son might have differed in that opinion, but it was my life, after all.

Beatrice swatted Sable's arm.

"Ouch!"

"Stop moving!"

"Why does the Tin Man have to be a woman anyway?" Sable grumbled.

"The Scarecrow, Tin Man, and Cowardly Lion are all women in our version."

"How very modern of you," Sable said.

"I think you've done an incredibly creative job with these costumes, Beatrice," I said, trying to distract her from Sable's protestations and continued wiggling.

"Why thank you, hon!" Beatrice glowed, pausing in her pinning long enough to bask in my admiration.

"I can't imagine what you must have thought when the director suggested you costume the play in steampunk."

"Actually, I suggested it," Beatrice said with a grin.

It wasn't too unbelievable, really. Beatrice's favorite part of costuming was the chance to be creative and to bring her own personality to each new endeavor.

The previous year, the community theater had performed Shakespeare's *Midsummer Night's Dream* in *space*. Beatrice's everyday ensembles had looked incredibly unique that summer. Steampunk *Wizard of Oz* didn't seem quite so crazy after that one.

"It's always such fun thinking outside the box," Beatrice went on. "I've had to think how I'd twist every little aspect, from turning Toto into a robo-dog to giving the flying monkeys and Wicked Witch of the West jetpacks."

I recalled Joseph's contribution, the jetpack he'd shown me at the shop.

"You and Joseph must have had a lot of time to connect while working on the show." I tried to use popcorn to cover the insinuation in my voice, but I guess Beatrice could hear through the crunching.

She turned and gave me a look. "I already told you: Joseph and I are just friends. I'm with Billy now. Joseph's been a great help with the mechanical side of things. But that's all. Maya can have her hardware man." She waved her hand as though throwing Maya a used handkerchief she no longer wanted. "We almost had to draft Joseph for the role of the Wizard, actually."

"But Joseph hates acting," Sable blurted, and then appeared surprised she'd said it.

I glanced at her.

"He's certainly better with his hands than with his mouth," Beatrice said.

Sable stiffened and gave Beatrice a look that said it all. Ever since Joseph had entered our conversations, Sable had seemed very eager to share what information she had of him. If I didn't know better, I'd guess there was yet another OBS member taken with the man.

"You know what I mean." Beatrice rolled her eyes at Sable. "If not Joseph, we probably would have gone with another gender-swapped role. It's so difficult to find men interested in community theater. Luckily, Billy appeared." She sighed like he'd shown up in nothing but a loin cloth riding a lightning bolt.

"Didn't you say he came from Broadway or something?" I asked.

Beatrice's eyes lit up at my question. "Yes! He was actually offered the role of the Phantom in *Phantom of the Opera*, but he turned it down!"

"Really?" Sable said, her disbelief evident in both syllables of the word.

"Yes, really," Beatrice repeated sarcastically. "He wanted to portray the Phantom accurately with an Italian accent but the director didn't appreciate his impression of Vito Corleone."

I almost choked on my popcorn.

"He did it for me and I thought it would have made what, in my opinion, is a rather boring production extremely entertaining!" Beatrice said enthusiastically.

Entertaining was not the word I would have chosen.

"He does the most wonderful accents," Beatrice went on. "You can ask him to imitate anyone and he can do it just like that!" Beatrice snapped her fingers, then gave a firm nod of her head toward the costume. "All right, hon, you can take it off now."

"Thank you," Sable sighed.

"Admit it: you stopped complaining because once it was on right, you found it quite comfortable, might even say you enjoyed it."

Sable rolled her eyes, but didn't respond.

She reached for the front of the busk and began to pull. Beatrice and I both leapt to stop her, but it was too late.

There was a twanging sound like an arrow flying from a bow. Something whizzed past my head, and the mirror shattered behind me.

{ 25 }

In Which Someone is to Blame

I hit the deck like it was the '50s and we were practicing duck-and-cover drills in school. Popcorn flew into the air and all over the floor. I remained there for several moments while my heart tried to find its way back up to my chest.

"What the—," Sable cried. "Goose, you all right?"

I couldn't speak. I took a deep breath of floor fibers and tried to settle my brain.

All I could think was that this must have been how that poor cockatiel felt right before the hatpin passed through his chest.

"If you'd waited half a moment I'd have told you I have to loosen the laces before you can take it off!" Beatrice wailed. "You can't just pull off a corset from the front!"

"How was I supposed to know that?" Sable yelled back.

"You've busted it!"

"No, I didn't. It's just some of the bits and bobs you pinned on."

Slings and Sparrows

"And the pins," I muttered from where I lay on the floor.

Amongst the popcorn and broken glass I could see numerous fallen pins from Beatrice's work that week.

Sable stepped off the stool and came to my side in two swift strides. Still holding the corset to her chest with one hand, she bent down and touched my shoulder with her other hand. I was forced to look her straight in the eyes.

"You all right, Goose? You look a bit shaken. It was just a flying bit of costume."

I nodded and pulled myself back into my chair. "My eyes flashed before my life," I said, then paused and tried again. "My life flashed before my eyes."

"I'm grateful you're not hurt," said Beatrice.

I smiled a little. "Just my pride."

"You move pretty quick for an old lady," Sable joked. "I swear you were on the floor quicker than Hugin on a fresh seed bag."

That got a small chuckle out of Beatrice and me, releasing the tension in the room.

I rubbed my temples where a headache was beginning.

"I think I just need some rest. I haven't slept well since Casper died, and then Tomi and Tuppence disappeared. Even with them safe now, I feel like I'm on pins and needles waiting for the next—well..." I waved my hand toward the mirror fragments behind me.

Sable patted my shoulder. "You should go home and lie down. Beatrice and I can finish up here. Probably best if there were fewer living targets sitting about." She winked at me and I wondered just how close she was to the mark.

"Oh, for heaven's sakes," Beatrice said, coming up behind Sable. "Like I was trying to tell you, this is simply what comes of unhooking the corset without loosening the laces. If you pull hard enough, the hooks detach from the whalebone entirely and go shooting across the room at audience members."

I leaned over to pick up one of the clasps from amongst the shattered mirror fragments and metal pins.

"Thank the Lord it happened here and not at the theater," Beatrice said, shaking her head. "Can you imagine what people would think if a part of my costume hurt someone?"

I left, as suggested, but for some reason, my steps drew me to the museum. Perhaps I just wanted to see my sister after my near-death experience, or maybe I knew I hadn't been the best at including her in my investigations.

I found Penny there, sure enough, cataloging away on the computer in the back room. I should probably mention that Penny did type with two hands on the keyboard. Henny had her own little station where she sat while Penny worked. She usually laid an egg while she waited.

With no rooster about, there was no worry that the eggs might be fertilized. Penny donated the daily eggs to the museum, selling them in a small fridge in the gift shop. May have nothing to do with history, but it was a way to make some money for a museum desperate for funds.

Tomi and Tuppence's eggs, on the other hand, which only appeared between May and September, went to Aunt Connie, who used them in her cooking.

I asked Penny once, before I got my own geese, if she thought it hurt Henny to lay eggs every day. Penny just laughed and said it was quite the opposite. Each Henny always seemed especially pleased with herself after laying an egg and would crow and flutter and strut about the room with great pride after laying.

"Have you managed to accomplish more today than you did on Saturday?" I asked by way of announcing my presence.

Penny jumped only slightly at my question. "Depends on what you think I set out to accomplish." She glanced at Henny as though to remind her she'd promised not to tell.

Henny didn't give up a thing; she looked to be half asleep in her nest in the corner.

Penny's screen, on the other hand, was showing a webpage with a man's face stamped across it in an excruciating number of poses.

Penny followed my gaze. "I think Billy Bacon designed the website himself," she said with a small smirk.

She scrolled down the page so I could admire just how many of his poses a girl could choose from to post on her wall.

"Jiminy crickets," I muttered. "You must have been sitting here for hours waiting for all those images to load. What a peacock. No wonder he and Beatrice get along."

Penny laughed lightly. "Now, now, Beatrice looks good compared to him."

She glanced toward the door of the office, which I'd left open, and nodded her head toward it. I shut it and pulled up a chair next to her little desk.

"So what's the scoop, Nellie Bly?" I asked.

"Who's—"

"Nellie Bly? A Gilded Age American female journalist."

"I should've guessed," Penny said with a smile. "All right, so it all began when I got this strange thought."

"That's how all the best ideas start," I said.

"Don't interrupt. I'll lose my train of thought," Penny said, waving at me impatiently. "So, I was thinking: What do we really know about all these new people in town? Specifically, the one person who keeps coming up in conversation between Beatrice and Maya. We know Joseph, or at least other people we trust do, so he's in the clear. But no one seems to know anything about Billy Bacon."

I almost said something but bit my lip and nodded instead.

"So I thought I'd do a little digging." She glanced at her screen. Apparently I'd been wrong to go to Jules for research assistance. All along, the best help was right here in front of me. Sometimes I was so blind to my sister's abilities.

"His full name is William *Tiberius* Bacon."

I couldn't help the snort that escaped. "Seriously?"

"Does this man look like he does anything *not* seriously?" Penny asked.

"True," I said. "Go on."

"He was born in 1931."

"So he's just a year older than me and Beatrice." I paused and recalled when *Star Trek* had first aired. "How did Bacon get Kirk's namesake before Captain Kirk himself came into being?"

"I'm certain he took on the middle name of his own accord," Penny said. "After all, he also claims he's related to Kevin Bacon."

"Isn't everyone related to Kevin Bacon by six degrees or less?" I asked, thinking about some silly thing Derrick had mentioned to me recently.

Penny gave me a look.

"Sorry, sorry." I smiled.

"As you know, he's playing the Wizard in our local production, and according to the *Gazette*, they're very excited about his performance because of his aptitude for accents."

"Beatrice mentioned something about that. So I take it he really does have past stage experience?"

Penny nodded. "Beatrice wasn't exaggerating. He really is Somebody."

She clicked over to a screen that listed his stage credits. She had to scroll many times to reveal them all. I could hardly believe that someone who'd once been in *Camelot* on Broadway with Julie Andrews would now perform with the Paca Springs community theater alongside high school students. Albeit, he'd never played a leading role. Perhaps he really had decided his talents would be more appreciated on a smaller stage, like Beatrice had said.

I looked more closely at the credits.

"Look at that," I said, jabbing at the screen with my finger.

"Don't touch!" Penny cried. "This thing's got every bit of cataloging I've done for the past two years. If I lost everything, I worry the museum wouldn't...consider me worth keeping..."

Her shoulders sagged and she looked at Henny in the corner. I took Penny's hand.

"They're not going to replace you. One day, the computers will all crash and everything will go back to the old card-catalog system. And when it does, no one will know where anything is or how to find it. They'll shake their heads and scream at the sky, 'If only Penny were still here!'"

Penny smiled and shook her head. "All right. Without touching the screen, what did you see?"

"The Kennedy Center. Maya's finale performance with Casper was held there."

"Interesting. Do you know when?" Penny asked.

"I've got it in my notes. Hold on." I reached into my pocket, grateful I'd shoved my notes in there on my way to Beatrice's, figuring I'd skim them while watching her work. I looked for the bottom of the list. "Let's see…uh…March of this year. Just before she moved in with us."

We both looked at the dates Bacon had been at the Kennedy Center. Sure enough, they'd both performed there on the same day in March.

"What are the chances of two professional stage performers finding their way to li'l ol' Paca Springs within two months of each other?" I asked. "Not very bloody likely, as Ruth would say."

{ 26 }

In Which We Wonder About Assassins

"It doesn't mean they knew each other," Penny protested. "Just because an actor performs on Broadway with Mandy Patinkin doesn't mean he knows him personally."

"But the Kennedy Center isn't Broadway."

"No, but it's close enough. Actors are in and out of shows so often I can't imagine they stay connected with every little extra. And Maya and Casper wouldn't have been performing *with* him necessarily. They'd have been just another act in a variety show, like vaudeville."

"Wait, did they ever perform together any other time?" I started perusing my notes as quickly as I could, wishing I'd taken the time to write down more details about each show.

"No need. I can look here," Penny said.

After a couple quick flicks of her fingers, we had our answer.

The computer screen filled with search results showing Casper and Bacon repeatedly performing in the same location, but only in the past year. Perhaps Billy Bacon's career had taken a dip and he'd had to leave Broadway to join the variety show circuit. It still didn't explain why they'd both ended up here, of all places, which wasn't on any circuit and barely had cellular phone service.

"Maya hasn't mentioned she knows Billy," I said. "Has she mentioned him to you?"

"Not at all." Penny shook her head. "Maybe this hasn't been about Joseph after all. Maybe it's about Beatrice's new man." She turned to me as she worked out her thought. "Maybe Maya and Billy were an item, and they had a fight and she ran away to the country, he followed her here to win her back, but she wouldn't leave and so he shot her bird—"

"Sounds like a romcom plot till that last part."

"You're right: that doesn't quite work," muttered Penny. "There's Beatrice. What if Beatrice got in the way and..." She trailed off because she knew as well as I did that it didn't explain why Billy or Beatrice would kill Casper.

"Unless...," Penny continued, "unless Beatrice has been lying this whole time and Billy isn't her new love interest. Perhaps instead, Billy's in pursuit of Maya, much to Beatrice's chagrin. She might have shot Casper to encourage Maya to leave town, leaving Billy all to her."

Once again, the clues seemed to indicate Beatrice as a suspect. And once again, I just couldn't believe it.

Yet again, I had just been shot at by her costume, so...

I realized I should probably tell Penny about my near-death escape.

"What if that was Beatrice's plan all along?" Penny asked once I'd finished.

"What do you mean?" I asked.

"What if she suggested steampunk in the first place so she could build contraptions into her costumes to spring an attack on someone onstage the night of the show?"

I laughed. "You make her sound like an assassin."

But Penny looked dead serious. "I'm dead serious," she said. "It doesn't have to be an actor or actress. It could be a patron of the show or a crew member. The point is: perhaps she's planned a costume 'accident.' Perhaps it wasn't the clasp that shot out, after all, but a pin. You said yourself the floor was covered with them. Could very well be you just happened to find a misleading clasp among the pins." She gasped and covered her mouth. "What if Casper's death was the trial run?"

I scratched my chin. "You mean, she wanted to see if her costume could fling a skewering hatpin across the room?" I shook my head at her wild idea. "What has she got against Maya?"

Penny raised an eyebrow at me. "Other than the fact that Joseph didn't show interest in her because of Maya? Or the fact that Maya might actually be in the way of Beatrice getting Billy?" Again she gasped and covered her mouth. "Maybe the costume malfunction is planned to hit *him* the night of the performance!"

"Do you know how absolutely *insane* you sound right now?" I whispered fiercely at her. "I cannot *believe* we're actually discussing this. I cannot believe *you're* actually suggesting this. It's one thing to suspect an OBS member of killing birds out of spite, but quite another to propose she's also about to murder a human being!"

"Shhhhh!" Penny said.

"*I am whispering!*"

Penny reached out and covered my mouth with her hand. We both eyed the door, waiting for someone to open it and ask why we were talking about murder in the backroom office.

Thankfully, no one did.

Penny let her hand drop.

"And another thing," I said in a whisper again. "Why would Beatrice use one of her own hatpins and then leave it behind, clearly linking Casper's murder to her?"

Penny pursed her lips and shook her head. "Don't you see? For that very reason. She knew we'd all assume it *wasn't* her because we'd all think she wouldn't be so stupid as to leave behind evidence like that."

I rubbed my forehead. "You're starting to sound like a mystery novel."

"At least one of us is," Penny said with a small sniff. "You'd think after two personal attacks you'd be more adamant about taking down the culprit."

"Two?"

Penny held up one finger. "Tomi and Tuppence." She held up a second finger. "You were just used as a test dummy yourself!" She slapped my shoulder.

"Ow," I said, rubbing the spot, though it had been no more than a tap.

"You're lucky you're alive, Goose," Penny said quietly. She put her hand on mine. "You were almost a second test *victim*."

I gave her hand a comforting squeeze, but I still didn't see it. "I just can't imagine Beatrice trying to kill me. Trying to kill anyone."

I didn't want to keep going down this train of thought. I despised feeling like I couldn't trust my closest friends.

"Sometimes it's those closest to us that we have the largest blinders about," Penny said softly.

"Is that from a book?"

Penny smiled. "No, that's pure Penny, thank you."

I returned her smile.

"You're never letting me out of your sight again, are you?" I asked, only half joking.

"Not until this show is over, at least," Penny said firmly. "And we are *not* getting front row seats."

{ 27 }

In Which We're Off to See the Wizard

After locking up the office and safely tucking Henny back under the right arm of Penny, we followed the yellow brick road to the school gym, which had been transformed into a theater for the weekend performance.

And by "transformed," I mean that there was a permanent stage at one end of the basketball court. All they had to do was raise the nets and boards and set up rows of folding chairs and *voila!* You had yourself the Paca Springs Community Theater.

They only put on one production a year, usually a musical, at the end of the summer. It was something for the kids to get involved in while school was out. Talent drifted in from all over, but usually included a range of kids to adults from all the other small towns within a thirty-mile radius.

Or from Broadway, as the case may be.

The first thing that went through my mind upon seeing Billy Bacon in the flesh was the description of Sam Spade in the opening of *The Maltese Falcon* by Dashiell Hammett: "He looked rather pleasantly like a blonde Satan." He even had the repeating V's from his widow's peak to his eyebrows, down to his nose, mouth, and chin.

From the moment I set eyes on him, I didn't trust him.

For one thing, he was looming over the director, waving his hands at poor, sweet Annabelle Blakely, who'd never hurt a fly. Annabelle was a teacher for special needs students who was now siphoning her talents for organization and her compassion for kids and adults into community theater. What she'd been able to accomplish in previous years blew the minds of the community. Between her and Beatrice's efforts, we were drawing enough crowds there were now rumors in town that, after this year, they might be able to build a real, live theater for future productions.

And right now this pillar of our community was being berated by a man who clearly equated himself with the character he was playing.

"When *I* was in New York, we did things very differently. An actor was permitted to share his opinions freely in New York, and the director always took them into consideration. I see it's very different in Paca Springs, where the director thinks she knows better than to listen to a man who's performed *Hamlet* in New York! Perhaps next year Paca Springs would be interested in hiring a man with more *experience* to lead their theater group. Perhaps next year I'll be in *your* place and you'll be in mine, *begging* me to listen to your opinion. And do you know what? I will listen to your opinion, because that's how a *professional* acts. Why when I was in New York—"

Surprisingly, it was Penny who beat me to the defense.

"Excuse me, Annabelle," Penny said loudly, clutching Henny like she was her source of power. "Do you have a few minutes?"

"Yes," Annabelle breathed. Her smile returned as she turned to Billy Bacon, saying, "We'll stick with the way it is for now, Billy. Thank you for your opinion." She turned her back on him in a clear dismissal and said, "How can I help you ladies?"

Bacon gave us a look of disbelief that we would *dare* interrupt his diatribe. Then he skulked off, no doubt to bother a set designer regarding something else he thought he knew better about.

"Thank you," Annabelle whispered, once he was out of earshot. "I'm remembering very quickly why I chose to become the director of a small-town community theater, rather than the larger stages."

"Like in New York?" I asked with a wink.

She smiled. "I've heard of prima donnas, of course, but I've never had the enlightening opportunity of working with one before."

Penny and I exchanged glances. There were certainly a few choice individuals in the community theater group that seemed to be working their way toward that level, but we couldn't imagine any of them daring to lecture Annabelle the way Bacon had just been doing.

"We're actually here to speak with Mr. Bacon," I said, "but no one should be allowed to talk to you like that, no matter who they are."

Annabelle waved a hand. "We're only a couple days from opening night. Tensions are perfectly normal. Everything always seems to go horribly wrong during tech week and then somehow, miraculously, it all comes together on opening night. Every. Single. Time," she punctuated.

I'd heard Beatrice mention that before. She seemed to thrive on the tension leading up to a performance. A show as crazy as this one was probably even more demanding than usual.

"So far, we have yet to make it all the way through the show in less than four hours," Annabelle said with a sigh, rubbing her temples. "But I promise that on Friday night, you'll be out of here in two and a half hours, including intermission."

I sure hoped so. Those folding chairs were almost as uncomfortable as the high school football stadium bleachers.

"Is there anything I can help you with?" Annabelle asked.

"Were you the one to cast Mr. Bacon as the Wizard?" Penny asked.

Annabelle nodded. "Partially, yes. We actually used a panel to cast: Beatrice, Lyle Smith the music director, and me. That way I can't be solely blamed for the roles they're given."

I smiled. Even with a panel, Beatrice usually said something along the lines of: "Annabelle Blakely thinks she's so great at casting, but she'll regret casting So-and-So as the Whatever, just you wait and see." But by the time the performance came around, Beatrice was always singing Annabelle's praises.

"Do you know what drew Mr. Bacon to audition for our little production in the first place?" I asked.

Annabelle shrugged. "He said he was getting tired of the politics in the larger arenas and was looking for something simpler. When I asked him if that meant he was hoping for a smaller role, however, he laughed in my face and shoved his list of stage credits under my nose."

"Why did you cast him if he was so rude about it?"

Annabelle sighed. "It's incredibly difficult to find male performers, especially with stage experience, willing to act for free in community theater."

"You're not paying him?" I asked in disbelief.

"Of course not," Annabelle said. "We're a non-profit organization. The money from ticket sales goes to funding the next year's performance. It's thanks to the success of *Midsummer Night's Dream* last summer that we're able to put on such a lavish production this year."

"So you're telling me a Broadway star is working for *free*?" This was getting weirder and weirder.

"I know!" Annabelle said, throwing up her hands. "That's partially why I put up with his...*opinions*. I figure we're lucky to have him."

"I bet he actually got fired from all those fabulous roles because of his attitude," I said. "and that's the real reason he's here, because no one would hire him."

Annabelle gave a small chuckle.

"Don't worry," Penny said, patting Annabelle on the arm with her free hand. "I promise you, nobody in Paca Springs will let someone like that take away your position as director of the community theater."

Annabelle smiled. "I sure hope not."

{ 28 }

In Which We Meet the Man Behind the Curtain

I decided then and there just exactly how I'd be interviewing Mr. Billy T. Bacon. Like any good goose, I rolled up my sleeves and prepared to hiss in his face if he so much as said one thing about New York or taking the theater from Annabelle.

Penny put a placating hand on my shoulder, however, and suggested maybe she should lead the questioning.

I cracked my knuckles in response. "Fine," I said. "I'll just be the muscle."

Penny bit back her laugh and gave Henny a knowing look. "Remember, there must be something decent about him. Beatrice likes him after all. And maybe Maya, too."

I gritted my teeth. "Let's just get this over with."

Once again, we were the saving angels, this time to a high schooler with a mic over her head and a clipboard in her hand. She looked about ready to melt into the floor like the Wicked

Witch as Bacon told her the proper way to remind an actor of his lines.

"When I was in New York—"

"Let me at him," I muttered as Penny said in a fawning tone, "Excuse me for interrupting once again, but we hadn't realized you were *The* William T. Bacon!"

I might've thought she was laying it on a bit thick, but in Bacon's case it was clear she'd laid it on not quite thickly enough.

"We're friends with Beatrice," she continued as the poor stagehand took this chance to disappear. "She said we just *had* to meet the most charming, debonair man this side of the Mason-Dixon."

"Ah," he purred, taking Penny's hand. "Any friends of Beatrice's are friends of mine." He lifted Penny's hand to his lips and actually kissed it. I knew she'd be washing the back of her hand forty-two times tonight. I tucked my own hands safely into my sweatpants pockets.

"My name's Penny and this is Henny." She raised the hen's wing to wave hello to Bacon. "And this is my sister, Goose."

"Beatrice didn't mention you two were a beautiful pair of twins!" Bacon said.

Gag. I was beginning to wonder if our questions were really worth all this.

"Is it true you're related to Kevin Bacon?" I asked.

"Naturally," he said. "Can't you tell?" He held his finger up to the cleft in his chin and turned his head this way and that, showing off his profile for us to admire.

"I think you're much better looking," Penny giggled.

I eyed her. I'd never known she could act so well. Maybe next year she'd need to try out for a role in *Arsenic and Old Lace*.

"Do tell me how I can be of assistance to you ladies. An autograph perhaps?" He whipped out a pen and headshot faster than a peacock unfurling his tail feathers.

"Oh, thank you," Penny tittered again. "Actually, we were wondering if you could tell us how such a *fine* actor as yourself came to be in Paca Springs?"

"Ah, well, I'm afraid I'm getting on in years..."

"Most certainly not," Penny said, actually patting him on the arm flirtatiously.

What on earth had happened to my anxiety-ridden little sister?

"You know, our friend also recently retired from the stage and settled here," I cut in, eager to get the questioning over with. "Perhaps you know her? Maya Grove?"

Bacon scratched his chin. "I'm sorry, the name doesn't ring a bell."

"Perhaps you've heard of her partner: Casper the Whistling Cockatiel?"

Bacon's eyes lit up. "Ah, yes! Of course! The little bird who whistles a happy show tune. He's here in Paca Springs?" He looked about as though expecting Casper to appear from behind my back.

"I'm afraid he *was* here," I clarified. "He recently passed."

Bacon's face fell. "How terrible." He clucked his tongue. "What a terrible, terrible loss for the variety show community."

"Indeed," I said. "Even more terrible, seeing as he was *murdered*."

Bacon's eyes went wide. I couldn't help but think that every one of his reactions so far had come across as rehearsed, but then again, maybe actors always seemed like they were acting. It wasn't like I'd met very many to draw a comparison.

"Murdered!" he cried.

"Yes," said Penny, squishing Henny and looking down at her sadly. "He was shot."

"Good heavens!" Bacon cried again, his hand flying to his chest.

Okay, now I knew he was acting. Nobody ever did that in real life.

"Are you sure it wasn't an accident, like Dorothy?" He waved toward the stage.

My eyes narrowed slightly. Interesting question. "We don't think so. It's not like someone dropped a house on him and stole his ruby slippers."

Bacon's eyebrows jumped slightly.

"He was skewered with a hatpin," Penny clarified.

Bacon shook his head melodramatically, his hand returning to his chest. "How horrible. What a way to go."

I half expected Penny to go on and warn Bacon that he might be next, but she didn't, and I was grateful. Something told me Bacon was the invincible-minded type who would refuse to believe that someone might be out to kill him. And it wasn't like we had any proof of our theory, just a hunch.

"So you didn't know Maya before?" I asked.

"I might have seen Casper perform once. I might have even performed with him at some time, but I never had the pleasure of meeting him in person." He sighed dramatically. "And now it seems I'm too late."

Penny echoed him with a sigh of her own.

"Will there be a funeral?" Bacon asked.

My eyes narrowed. Why would he want to know that?

"No, she had a personal funeral, just her and Casper," Penny said.

"Too bad, too bad. I would have liked the chance to share my memories of him."

"I thought you'd never met him," I said.

Bacon waved his hand. "Oh, but memories come in so many forms." With a great flourish, he signed his name on his headshot and handed it to Penny. "Now, if you'll excuse me, ladies, I really must begin preparing for our evening dress rehearsal."

"Thank you!" Penny said.

"Good luck!" I said with a grin, perfectly aware that it was bad luck to say "good luck" to actors.

Bacon winced, but didn't correct me. Instead, he slipped behind the stage curtain with an ostentatious wave of his hand worthy of one of Beatrice's peacocks.

"That was rather thoughtful of him to want to attend Casper's funeral," Penny said, giving Henny a pat.

I bit my lip. Something didn't seem right to me about that concern, but I didn't have anything other than a gut feeling to go on about that, so I let it slide.

"I suppose we'd better get home and check on Tomi and Tuppence," I said. "If they've disappeared again, the full fury of Goose will be raining down on all of Paca Springs."

{ 29 }

In Which Something Goes Honk in the Night

I startled awake in the middle of the night, *The Prestige* lying open on my chest where it had settled after I'd fallen asleep reading "just one more page."

I was absolutely certain someone was in my room.

My heart raced, but I refused to be cowed. I grabbed the baseball bat I kept by my bed for such emergencies and swung it with all my might just to be sure, before even turning on the light.

No one was there.

"*Hiss! Honk! Honk! Hiss!*"

There it was again!

I leapt out of bed and flung open my door, bat prepped at my side like a gun.

I couldn't see anybody, but I heard two more doors down the hall squeak open.

"Goose?" Penny called out.

"Penny? Maya?" I responded. "Everyone all right?"

"We're fine," Maya said. "What is it?"

"I heard something," I said. "Stay in your rooms. I'll handle it."

My heart pounded as I slowly made my way down the stairs and toward the kitchen. Now that I knew it wasn't Maya or Penny, I had no qualms about swinging my bat around in the darkness.

"You mess with the Old Birds, you get the Goose!" I cried out, bursting into the kitchen and flinging on the light.

I'll admit, it had sounded better in my head. Thankfully, there was nobody there to hear me.

"I think it came from the sunroom," Maya called out, leaning over the stairway bannister.

I could just make out Penny in her nightdress at the top of the stairs with Henny in her arms as I crossed the foyer into the living room.

"Hello?" I called, like every other idiot who's ever walked into a dark room in a movie, as though the person hiding there would be dumb enough to call back, "I'm over here with my chainsaw!"

I flipped on a lamp as I passed the couch. There were no more sounds, but I still moved hesitantly.

I opted for silent but deadly as I entered the sunroom, flinging the door open and throwing my bat through ahead of me.

Clang! Grunt. *Clash!*

"Goose!" Penny cried behind me.

"I'm all right," I grumbled from the floor.

She flipped on the light in order to better see my sprawled form prostrate before her.

"Goose!" she cried again, setting down Henny and reaching for my hand. "Honey, are you all right?"

"Yeah, yeah. Just tripped over Casper's birdcage."

"What was it doing on the floor?" Penny asked. She helped me slowly to my feet and then into a nearby chair when I yelped in pain.

"My stupid ankle twisted a little when I hit the cage. I'll be all right in a minute, just need to catch my breath."

Maya appeared in the doorway and went straight for the cage—not poor little me.

"You've damaged it!" Maya cried.

Penny glared at her. "It's not her fault! Why would you leave Casper's cage on the floor?"

"I didn't!" Maya yelled back. "I left it—" Her finger pointed toward where we'd both seen Casper's cage just a few days ago.

"Why did it fall?" Maya asked, going to the bird stand and inspecting it before lifting Casper's cage back to its proper place. She pouted. "It's completely broken. Just look at this. A whole piece fell off the bottom."

Penny glanced about. "I wonder what knocked it over."

As if in answer, we all turned as Tomi and Tuppence waddled in through the open backyard door, the cool summer air wafting in with them.

"Did you two make this mess?" I asked them sternly.

"Honk, honk, honk!" they cried in unison.

"What did you do?" I asked.

"Honk, honk, honk!" They waddled toward me and then circled back out the door, almost like they wanted me to follow them.

I glanced at Penny, who seemed to read my mind. She handed me my bat and scooped up Henny.

I tried to stand. My ankle twinged in pain, but not so badly I couldn't put my weight on it. I hobbled toward the door.

"Did you leave the door open?" I heard Penny whisper to Maya behind me.

"No," she whispered back. "Did you?"

I flipped on the back porch light and took a gander.

"Nothing out here but two worried geese," I muttered.

I didn't mention that I couldn't be absolutely certain thanks to night blindness. It was pitch black past the arc of the porch light—anyone could be standing just beyond its glow. Then again, the fact that Tomi and Tuppence had stopped honking and were now waddling stoically into the night seemed to be a positive sign that there was nothing hiding in the dark. At least, not anymore.

I was brave, but I wasn't stupid. There was no way I was going out into that darkness with nothing but a bat and a turned ankle.

"I woke up to Tomi and Tuppence honking and hissing at someone," I said, coming back inside. "Better than guard dogs, those two."

I closed the door behind me, flipping the lock but leaving the light on outside.

"So there really was an intruder," Maya murmured.

I looked around the sunroom. Nothing seemed to have been taken, not that there was much worth stealing: just some wicker furniture, a few house plants, and Casper's birdcage.

"The intruder broke in to mangle Casper's old birdcage?" I asked skeptically. "Why on earth would someone do that?"

Penny and I looked at Maya, but she just shrugged. "Don't look at me. I have no idea."

"Well, clearly someone has it out for Casper or you—or both of you," I said, hobbling slowly back toward the living room. "I'm going back to bed. We can't figure this out tonight. We can call the police in the morning, if you want, but I think they'll just laugh in our faces. In the meantime, I suggest we all get some rest so we can meet the problem with fresh minds in the morning."

But there was no way I was going back to sleep.

I tossed and turned, a million thoughts running through my brain. Finally, I threw back the sheets and went downstairs to see if we had any valerian root to make some tea. Sable was the one who'd put me on to this natural remedy. Even with a hot cup of tea between my hands, however, the questions wouldn't stop circling.

Was it really worth it? Did I even *want* to know who'd killed Casper?

All my investigations had turned up so far was more pain, more complications. We'd been living such a simple, beautiful life until Casper's demise. Now Tomi and Tuppence were at risk, I was at risk, our whole household was at risk. Part of me—a large part of me—didn't feel like all of that, plus the growing distrust of my dearest friends, was worth discovering the murderer of a cockatiel.

Slings and Sparrows

I believed Maya when she said she didn't know why these things were happening. I could tell she was scared. Scared enough to try to run away.

Obviously there was something in her past which had caused her to run to Paca Springs in the first place. She'd most likely thought a small town would protect her, but it hadn't. In fact, it had done the exact opposite: it had provided the killer with an easier target. In a city, she might've been able to blend in amongst thousands of people, but in a town of a thousand, where everyone knew everyone else, it was much more difficult for a remarkable woman and her whistling cockatiel to disappear.

We had to figure out who was behind this. For Maya's sake. Otherwise, I was afraid she'd be on the run for the rest of her life.

{ 30 }

In Which a Thief is Discovered

"My back is killing me," I stated at breakfast the next morning.

"My neck," Maya said, stretching it from side to side.

"My arm," Penny said.

"Can't imagine why," I muttered, giving Henny the stink eye. "I definitely injured myself when I tripped on that dratted cage last night."

"You said you twisted your ankle," Penny said.

"Yeah, yeah, but this morning it's my back that hurts."

"Probably because you landed on your bat when you fell," Maya said. "Do you always sleep with a bat in your room?"

"There's usually two to three single women-of-a-certain-age living in this house," I said. "We never lock our doors 'cause we simply never have, so yeah, I sleep with a bat in my room." I took a sip of coffee. "Though I tell you the first thing I'm doing today is going down to the hardware store and buying some top-notch locks."

The other two nodded in approval.

"At least no one was hurt," Penny said.

I gave her a look over my mug. "No one?"

"Well, other than you. But it could've been worse!" Penny took a sip of her morning cup of tea and ran her hand over Henny at her side. "Do you think someone broke in and *accidentally* bumped into Casper's cage in the dark? Like you did?"

"It certainly makes more sense than someone breaking in merely to go after Casper's cage in the first place." I looked at Maya.

"Why would they? I still don't know," Maya said apologetically. "I wracked my brain all night, and I couldn't think of any reason. I mean, it's not like the cage is made of gold."

"And they didn't take it," Penny pointed out. "They just broke it apart."

"Yeah, that's what makes it even stranger," I said. "It's like they were looking for something."

"Do you think the person who killed Casper did it so they could search the cage? Maybe they were interrupted and had to leave before the job was done?" Penny asked Maya. "So they came back?"

Maya shrugged. "There was nothing in the cage but newspaper and bird droppings."

"When you picked it up last night, it looked like someone had removed the bottom."

"Yeah," Maya said, "which wouldn't be easy to do. They'd have to unscrew it."

"That'd be pretty difficult to do if there was still a bird living in it," Penny said.

"True," Maya admitted.

I thought Penny might be on to something.

"Maya, have you ever heard of Billy Bacon?" I asked.

Maya rolled her eyes. "Of course I have. You were there when Beatrice was using him as an excuse for no longer being interested in Joseph."

"So you hadn't heard of him before Saturday?"

Maya shook her head and took a sip of coffee. "No, should I have?"

"We learned yesterday that you two might have actually crossed paths several times this last year. On the variety show circuit."

"I think I'd remember if I'd ever shared the stage with a 'Billy Bacon.' That's a pretty unforgettable name. What's his talent?"

"Being a royal pain, as far as I can tell," I said. Penny kicked me under the table. "He might not have performed *with* you, just in the same location at the same time."

"You might have seen him at Casper's finale performance, actually," Penny said. "You were both at the Kennedy Center."

Maya nodded. "I'm sure we were, but The Kennedy Center is a performing arts center with something like nine different performance spaces. While I was on one stage, Billy Bacon might have been on a separate one without us ever crossing paths."

"Oh," Penny and I said.

"Billy Bacon," Maya repeated. Suddenly, her eyes lit up. "Wait, I do remember him."

"He's pretty hard to forget. He comes across all dashing and debonair but really he's slick as snot," I said. Penny tried to kick me again, but I'd moved my leg out of her range.

"No, no, I don't remember him that way. I remember him because of the theft."

"The theft?" Penny and I repeated in unison.

"Yeah, yeah." Maya set down her coffee. "The night of Casper's finale performance: we weren't allowed to leave afterward because everyone was being questioned. Some lady had lost her ruby necklace worth something like half a million dollars."

I nearly choked on my coffee. "Who wears jewelry worth that much out in public?"

Maya shrugged. "It's the Kennedy Center. It's one of the premiere stages in the D.C. area. They host Broadway performances, ballets, symphonies, and performers from Johnny Carson to Mary Martin to Aretha Franklin."

"Aunt Connie talks about seeing *Rigoletto* there once a couple years back. I bet it was amazing." Penny sighed.

"Wow. Guess I need to get out more," I muttered. "A half-a-million-dollar necklace. Did they ever find the thief?"

"That's what made me realize I've heard Billy Bacon's name before," Maya said. "He was one of the leading suspects."

While my jaw dropped, my mind kept working. Why had they suspected Bacon at the time of the theft? Had he been implicated before? Perhaps that incident hadn't been the first time a pricey bit of jewelry had gone missing after one of his performances? Perhaps that was the real reason why he was here in Paca Springs, to let the heat die down?

Just then, the wheels in my head clunked into something. "He actually did seem a mite jumpy when I jokingly said that Casper wasn't killed for his *ruby* slippers. Maybe I was closer to the truth than I realized."

Penny looked at me. "What do you mean?"

I turned to Maya. "The removed birdcage bottom: was there an empty space under there?"

Maya nodded.

"What're you thinking, Goose?" Penny asked.

"I was just wondering if something might've been hidden in the cage itself."

"Something someone wanted to sneak out of a theater without being caught, you mean?" Penny asked, getting my drift.

"Yeah," I said. "Something like a half-a-million-dollar ruby necklace."

{ 31 }

In Which We Tell Beatrice What We've Learned

"Well, I guess that would explain why a Broadway actor suddenly showed up in Paca Springs to join the summer community theater production," Penny murmured.

"Bacon must've realized there was no getting out of the theater that night with the necklace," I mused aloud. "He looked about for some place to hide it—maybe ran into several different dressing rooms trying to come up with a plan, or maybe luck led him to the best spot first. He sees the empty birdcage and thinks, *Perfect. I'll hide it in there. The police would never think to look in the bottom of a birdcage. In a few days, once the heat has died down, it will be a simple matter of tracking down the owner, wangling my way into her heart, and gaining access again. Then I'll help myself to the necklace and be on my way. No one will ever know!*"

"That was a perfect imitation!" Penny cried.

"Why thank you, thank you very much!" I said, offering my best Elvis impression next.

Maya didn't seem quite so impressed.

I cleared my throat and continued. "But a problem arises: he learns that night was Casper's last performance. Tracking down where you're headed next isn't going to be as easy as he thought. Somehow, though, he figures out you're in Paca Springs, and there just happens to be a local community theater. So what could be simpler than offering his services while he waits for the opportune moment?"

Maya frowned. "But why kill Casper? Couldn't he have just waited for the cage to be empty?"

"Did you ever once leave the cage empty and let Casper fly free? I mean, outside of the sunroom?"

Maya bit her lip and shook her head. "I see what you mean."

"If that's where the necklace was hidden, in the bottom of Casper's cage, that would explain why Bacon was so interested to learn about Casper's death."

"Except if he *learned* about Casper's death, that implies he didn't know about it in the first place, so he's not the murderer," Penny pointed out. She could poke holes in my extremely logical deductive reasoning like a hen pecking for grit.

I held up my hand like Hamlet holding the skull of poor Yorrick. "He's an actor!" I proclaimed, returning to my Bacon impression. "He was obviously lying about several things when we spoke to him. Clearly one of them was that he didn't 'know' about Casper's death."

"You told him about it?" Maya asked.

Penny and I shrugged.

"We didn't see the harm in it at the time," I said. "We were trying to find out if you two had known each other."

"We thought," Penny blushed, "the two of you might have been an item, that maybe he'd come to town in search of you."

"Ha!" Maya laughed. "That's rich."

"Well, he certainly is if he's got that necklace," I said. "I bet he's skipped town by now."

"Not while his audience awaits his sterling rendition of the Wizard, surely!" Penny said sarcastically.

"We should ask Beatrice if she's heard anything. She'd be the first to hear if he's left for good." Maya gasped slightly. "What if he's planning to take her with him?"

Penny and I exchanged a look.

"Nah," I said, waving a hand dismissively.

"Unless he proposed with the necklace, concealing where it came from," Penny pointed out. "She might think he's just being incredibly romantic and run away with him."

I had to admit, she had a point.

"Perhaps I'd better swing by, just to be sure," I said, scraping my chair back.

"I'll come with you," Penny said. I was reminded of her declaration never to let me out of her sight between now and the closing performance on Sunday night.

We dressed and headed over to Beatrice's, leaving Maya to continue packing. She suggested we take the cage with us, in case Beatrice required proof of our adventures the previous night. We didn't argue. She was probably right.

As we stepped outside, I was glad to see Tomi and Tuppence honking merrily along the pond's edge. We walked over to say good morning and they ended up tagging along, waddling at my heels like they were as concerned for my safety as Penny.

"You're the ones who got locked in a shed," I reminded them.

"Honk," Tuppence said, looking at Tomi like it was her fault.

"Ho-onk," she replied, shaking her beak back and forth.

"Ah," I said, knowingly.

"What did they say?" Penny asked, being only fluent in chicken, not goose. It's somewhat similar but you've got to get a feel for the dialect.

"Tuppence admitted they did look a bit silly getting themselves locked up. Then Tomi said, 'Partnership may sometimes stumble, but it always finds its way back on track.'"

Penny laughed. "Do they ever speak in quotes that aren't from Tommy and Tuppence novels?"

"Where would be the fun in that?"

When we reached Beatrice's yard, the peacocks and peahens were gathered to the north, stretched out across the lawn in an evenly-spaced V and slowly working their way up the yard toward the house. I think they did that to ensure not a single delicious bug was missed between them.

We knocked on the door but there was no response. We both leaned in, but couldn't hear the sewing machine going. Neither could we see her when we peeked through the windows.

"Beatrice?" I called out, knocking again.

Still no answer. We circled to the back door, which opened on the kitchen. I knocked and called out again before we let ourselves in.

Not a sound.

"Beatrice?"

We timidly walked through the house, but there was no sign of her.

Slings and Sparrows

"She must be down at the theater?" Penny suggested.

"I hope so," I said. "I hope we're not too late and that she hasn't run off with that loser."

"What loser?" Beatrice asked. We both spun around, clutching our chests. Beatrice laughed, removing her earphones and pulling her Walkman CD-player from her pocket. "See! Now you know how it feels when you surprise me at my sewing machine."

"Where were you?" I asked. "We were calling and calling."

"You must have just missed me. I went for a little early morning walk to get my energy up." She was already dressed with her hair done and makeup on, though her skirts were pinned up so I could see her anachronistic muck boots. Her eyes sparkled. "We're in the final stretch now."

"Final stretch?" Penny asked.

"For the show, hon. Tomorrow's opening night! Can you believe it? I hardly slept last night, I'm so excited." She pointed to the cage in my hand. "What's that?"

"Casper's birdcage," I said, holding it up.

"What happened to it?" she asked, taking in the bent bars and the loose panel hanging from the bottom. "Did that happen when he..." She didn't finish.

"No, no," I said. "It happened last night."

"We didn't get much sleep last night, either," said Penny.

We told her about our break-in, which she took in with wide eyes.

"But that's only half of it," I finished. "We're pretty sure we know who it was, and why."

"Who?"

"Billy Bacon," I said.

Beatrice tilted her long neck back and laughed. "Oh, come now, you two," she said, swatting her hands at us. "Stop pulling my leg."

"We're serious," Penny said. "Maya says he was a suspect in a jewel theft, and we think he must've hidden a stolen ruby necklace worth half-a-million in the bottom of Casper's cage."

"That's why he's here. He's been searching for Maya ever since she retired and now he's found her."

Beatrice held up a hand. "Wait, next you're gonna tell me he killed Casper, too."

"He did!" I said. "In order to get access to the cage, he had to make sure Casper was out of the way."

"That's ridiculous," Beatrice said, no longer laughing. "You two should be ashamed of yourselves."

Penny and Henny certainly looked it, but I wasn't about to let go. This was for Beatrice's own good.

"Beatrice, we're concerned about you. You don't know who this man really is. He might've even skipped town already."

"Balderdash," Beatrice said, her cheeks warming. "He's done no such thing. He'd never leave before the performance. What proof do you have of any of this?"

I held up the cage.

"That's it? A broken cage?" She glared from me to Penny and back again. "No torn bits of his Wizard costume? No missing handkerchief? No fingerprints or bootprints? You two are just about the worst detectives I've ever heard of. And I've about had it with your accusations. First against me and now against Billy? I thought you were my friends."

She whirled around and stomped her little booted feet out the kitchen door, letting it slam behind her.

Penny and I avoided each other's eyes. We both knew Beatrice had a point. But we also knew we were trying to protect her.

"Wait until after the show is over," Penny murmured. "Like Annabelle said, tensions run high during tech week, and this mystery isn't helping matters."

"If Bacon doesn't leave by Monday, *without* Beatrice," I growled, "I'll chase him out of town myself." With Tomi and Tuppence's help, of course.

{ 32 }

In Which I Get a Call From My Son

When the phone rang that afternoon, I half expected it to be Beatrice calling in tears, saying that Bacon had run away and the show was ruined because who on earth could they ever get this late in the game to play the Wizard...

But it was just my son.

"Hey, Mom," he said.

I cannot begin to describe how good it was to hear his voice at that moment. A huge wave of relief rolled through me and I almost burst into tears—which I absolutely, positively never do.

Unless I'm watching a *Thin Man* film, but then it's laughing tears.

"So, how are things?" he asked.

Before I could stop myself, I'd told him everything that had happened since Saturday in one long, unending sentence about as tangled as the phone cord.

"Woah. Usually when I ask, 'How are things?' you just say, 'Nuthin' much,' and we move on. Jiminy Christmas, Mom, I wish you'd called me sooner."

"Why? There's no way you could've helped."

"Doesn't matter. You're my mom and I want to know what's going on with you. I shouldn't be the one calling you all the time. Sometimes you could call me, you know."

I smiled. Derrick was a great kid. Even at forty-one.

"I was calling to find out if we could visit in three weeks, but maybe I ought to look at flying out there sooner."

Derrick, his wife, and three kids lived in Colorado Springs, which was just a flight away, but it seemed ever so much farther sometimes. Like right now.

"No, no, it's okay," I said, winding the phone cord around my fingers. "We're fine."

"I'll look into this Billy Bacon guy for you, okay? And if I find anything suspicious I'll let you know."

"Thanks, but you don't have to—"

"Let me do something, okay? I'm stuck out here in the Springs burning daylight while my mom deals with murdered birds, stolen necklaces, and things that go bump in the night."

"And steampunk *Wizard of Oz*."

"That goes without saying." He chuckled lightly. "Only Paca Springs community theater would try something so daring. Maybe I'll fly out just to catch the performance. How's Aunt Penny doing with it all? I bet poor Henny's 'bout lost all her feathers from all the worried kneading she's probably getting."

I laughed at that thought. "She's actually doing much better than I thought she'd be. I think focusing on the mystery is keeping us both from losing it. If we took a step back and really examined this week, I think we'd both take up your offer for yinz to move in and take care of our nerve-wracked old bodies."

"I'm serious, Mom. Do you need me to come?"

I took a deep breath and looked out the window toward the pond. Tomi and Tuppence were kicking and splashing each other like my grandkids when they came to visit.

"I'm not gonna lie," I said. "I'm tempted to say yes, but by the time you got here, I think it would all be over."

"You don't think someone in the OBS is to blame?"

"No, I really do think it's Billy Bacon."

"Is it because the facts seem to point to him or because you really want it to be him, so it's not one of your friends?"

"Right in one, kid," I said. "How'd you get so smart?"

"Smart parenting."

I smiled. How'd we get so lucky?

"Woah!" Derrick suddenly exclaimed.

"What?"

"This guy really likes the look of himself, doesn't he?"

"Billy Bacon?"

"Oh my gosh, his middle name is Tiberius? Seriously? Where did this guy come from?"

"Now you see what I've been up against. This world gets crazier by the day." I laughed. "I didn't realize when you said you'd look into Bacon you meant right away."

"Might as well. Got my computer right here. Already had the internet dialed up and everything, so I'm gonna look up Casper the Whistling Cockatiel, too. This Billy Bacon page is taking far too long to load with all these pictures. I'll have to come back and take more of a look at him later."

"When you look up Casper, there should be a link that takes you to his official websi—"

"He sings show tunes!"

"Yeah."

"Seriously? He once whistled 'Bring Him Home' from *Les Mis* with Colm Wilkinson himself?" Derrick gave his own whistle of admiration.

"Somehow I have a difficult time believing a cockatiel could upstage Colm Wilkinson. The man sings that song so perfectly I cry just thinking about it. I'm pretty sure I wouldn't have been the only one in the audience shouting at the bird to shut up." I leaned back in my chair and glanced around the living room, hoping Maya hadn't returned.

"It's a very impressive résumé—for a bird. I can see why he'd be popular. How old is his trainer?"

"Maya?"

"Yeah."

"Somewhere around sixty."

"Wow. She looks like she's my age."

"I know. She dyes her hair."

"No need to get defensive, Mom. I wish there were more close-up pictures of Casper. Lots of photos of him on stage, but...I don't suppose a bird would have a headshot."

"I read in an interview that he got upset with too many visitors, so Maya never allowed one-on-one meets with him."

"Understandable. You only have to watch every episode of *America's Funniest Home Videos* or animal encounters on a talk show to see how important it is for a performing animal to be in the best of spirits to do what his trainer wants him to do."

"Yeah." The image of Tomi and Tuppence performing before a live studio audience flittered across my mind's eye. They'd cause a riot.

"Wow, they went all over, didn't they? What a life! Always on the move. Why did Maya retire him anyway?"

"Probably because he was getting old, for a cockatiel."

"How old was he?" Derrick asked.

"I think she said she found him seventeen years ago. I didn't know cockatiels lived that long until she told me."

"Not surprised. Any bird living the cushy life of a pet is bound to live longer than average," Derrick said. "Too bad he and Billy Bacon never teamed up. They'd have made quite the pair. They both look about as full of themselves."

I laughed again. "Gosh, it's good to talk to you, buddy. The next time we have a murder mystery on our hands, I'll be sure to call you sooner. I could've used this all week."

"Sure thing, Mom. Let me know how I can help."

"I just feel like we're missing something. There's some piece that's not fitting correctly."

"Maybe what you think is a water piece is actually a part of the sky?" Derrick suggested.

"Or vice versa."

"Just assume everyone's lying, Mom. Isn't that something one of your detectives would say?"

"Yes, but these are my friends."

"And how often have friends and family been the culprits in your novels?"

"I—"

"My point exactly. Let it rest, Mom. Tomi and Tuppence are fine and Maya's leaving, which means she's most likely taking the problem with her. Let her go and let it go. I'll see you in three weeks. Love ya!"

And that was it. But I wasn't giving up that easily. Tomorrow, I'd be attending the opening night production of the Paca Springs *Wizard of Oz*. I had plenty of thoughts to keep me busy till then.

{ 33 }

In Which We Travel to Oz

There was nothing quite like the anticipatory quiet of a theater just before a show began, especially on opening night.

There we all were, all the suspects, sprinkled throughout the gym's folding chairs. It was almost like the scene at the end of so many Golden Age detective novels, where the detective called everyone together so he could reveal everything he'd uncovered in perfectly detailed order.

Aunt Connie and her brood made up at least a quarter of the audience. Ruth and Alice were seated with friends in the third and sixth rows. Beatrice and Joseph were backstage dealing with any last-minute costume or mechanical hiccups. And the wonderful, marvelous, magnificent William T. Bacon was said to have been in his dressing room practicing vocal warm-ups since four o'clock. Beatrice had made sure Annabelle told us, refusing to tell us herself.

Sable was seated with us, melting into the shadows of the back row in her black jean jacket, t-shirt, and matching jeans.

Slings and Sparrows

Penny had still argued against sitting in the front row, although Beatrice had reserved seats for us there—before we'd accused her boyfriend of theft and avicide. Now the front row was filled with various other cast family members, none of whom struck me as being in danger of a flying costume malfunction. Joseph and Billy Bacon were certainly within range, but since the discovery of the stolen necklace, I was beginning to think the whole corset thing had just been a red herring.

The only OBS member missing was Maya, who'd opted to stay home and finish packing. She'd told me she would catch the closing night's performance before she headed out of town on Monday.

As the lights went down, I settled in for two and a half hours—who was I kidding? I knew it was going to be at least three with the intermission—of distracting storytelling.

Boy, was I wrong.

The ruby slippers on Jennifer Meyer's feet were dazzling. Beatrice had really outdone herself with the costuming. Jennifer's blue-and-white-checkered corset gave a nod to the Dorothy of the film, while her navy blue overskirt was tucked up to reveal white petticoats underneath. The brown hat she wore pinned to her pompadour hairstyle also bore a pair of goggles, which came in handy during the tornado sequence.

Since the novel was first published in 1900, I began to wonder if a "steampunk" version of the story wasn't precisely what L. Frank Baum was going for when he originally wrote it. One of the sequel books had even featured a clockwork mechanical man.

The ruby slippers sure sparkled like a necklace, and for a moment I almost thought maybe Beatrice had stolen the necklace and turned it into slippers in order to hide it "in plain sight." But the more I looked at the shoes the more it was apparent that they were just covered in glitter.

I adjusted myself in my seat and tried to fall into Oz the way Dorothy was doing, pushing the details of Casper's murder to the back of my mind. Unfortunately, those same details insisted on muscling their way to the forefront with every line and action on stage.

Glinda's magical appearance on a "steam train," which was actually a decorated bubble-blowing machine, made me think about Joseph at the hardware store. I would've bet good money he had something to do with its construction. He had clearly been interested in Maya; his flustered countenance had implied a tender heart when it came to her and her whistling cockatiel. But that didn't mean Maya had been wrong about his interest in Beatrice as well.

The Scarecrow, Tin Woman, and Cowardly Lioness—all young ladies in corsets, as Beatrice had said—brought to mind the numerous other ladies involved in the mystery. It had never occurred to me to run a background check on the other OBS members, but after all, they were women I would most likely be spending the rest of my life with. Now I wondered if I mightn't have been a bit hasty in assuming none of them had anything to hide.

The main characters continued to dance their way toward Oz. With every step the Tin Woman took, I tensed, waiting for some bit of her costume to fly off and skewer someone.

Slings and Sparrows

But nothing happened and once again, as she left the stage, I relaxed and tried to shake out the tension in my limbs. Henny always let out a sighing cluck as I did this, so I figured Penny was probably squeezing her tightly at the same times for the same reasons.

During intermission we stood and stretched. Sable went to grab a cup of fruit punch from the concession stand. I considered getting some popcorn, but that only made me think of the popcorn sprinkling the ground after I was almost hit by shooting corsetry.

"No one's died yet," I muttered into Penny's ear.

She nodded grimly. "I hate this. I'm an absolute wreck." Her hand ran worriedly down Henny over and over again, from her head to her tail feathers. "I'm tempted to leave but then I'm afraid I'll miss something."

"Yeah," I agreed. "I'm only half paying attention to the show. The other half of me is working through clues, hoping for connections."

The second act opened and there he was, the Great Wizard of Oz himself. Bacon had chosen to do a ridiculous Christopher Walken impression behind the mechanical steampunk face, which moved and gyrated like something from a Broadway production. It was too bad: Joseph had more skill than I'd given the man credit for, and his Wizard's face deserved a better voice coming out of it.

It appeared Beatrice had been right and Bacon really hadn't left town. But if he'd broken into the house to steal the necklace back, why hadn't he? Was starring as the Wizard in a local production really worth staying? Or was it Beatrice? Had he fallen in love and his foolish heart couldn't leave her?

I hoped he kept his mitts off her, personally. I knew she could do better. She may've been a bit of a strutting peahen sometimes, but she was my friend, and my heart ached to think of her leaving us, especially over a rift like this.

Just then, a new thought shot through my brain like the Wicked Witch of the West on her mechanical broomstick.

What if the ruby necklace *hadn't* been in the bottom of Casper's birdcage? What if it had been as empty as the Tin Woman's corseted chest?

That would explain why Bacon was still here. He hadn't found what he'd been looking for. Or maybe nothing had ever been hidden in there, and once again we'd been duped by a red herring?

But someone *had* broken in that night. Someone *had* banged up Casper's cage and opened the false bottom. So there must have been *something* hidden there.

Whatever it was, where was it now?

{ 34 }

In Which the Great Detective Leaves Us Hanging

The show ended and we all rose to our feet to give a standing ovation. The acting might have been below the standard for say, The Kennedy Center, but for small-town theater it had been pretty good. The costuming and sets had been incredible, and they, if nothing else, deserved our appreciation.

The murmur of theater-goers filled the gym as the cast came down the steps at the sides of the stage to greet family and friends. Penny, Sable, and I milled in the back, eventually making our way out into the cool night, where I relaxed a little more.

Night air always rejuvenates me. I took a deep, slow breath in and out.

"Someone's stressed," said Alice as she joined us with Ruth.

They both looked far more enthused about the show than I felt. As the cast had lined up for bows at the very end—Billy Bacon giving the grandest bow of them all and kissing his hands out to the audience as though he were the star of the show—I'd almost had it. The pieces of our mystery had almost come together.

"Just a little stressed," I said. "It's on the tip of my brain. The answer to all of it."

"To what?" Alice asked.

"You've found the sparrow with the bow and arrow?" Sable asked. She really did get me. I hoped she wasn't the culprit.

"Yes, almost…it has something to do with the Wizard."

"The Wizard?" Ruth asked, looking over her shoulder at the gym doors where patrons of the arts continued to flow out.

"And ruby slippers and Lamb Chop and Julie Andrews."

"What are you talking about?" Alice asked, a look of great concern for my mental health crossing her face.

"Don't interrupt, her gray cells are working," Penny said. "Go on, Goose. You can figure it out."

I looked from Penny to Sable to Henny and back again.

"You can help a little. What did you just say?"

"I just asked if you'd found the sparrow who killed Casper yet," Sable repeated.

"That wasn't it."

"You were talking about the production," Ruth offered.

"About Beatrice's beautiful costumes," said Penny.

"And Joseph's mechanical contraptions," said Sable.

I snapped my fingers. "Yes, something about Joseph."

"You think Joseph is the murderer?" Sable asked.

"No," I muttered, that hadn't been it. "I don't have a motive for him."

"Perhaps it was an accident," suggested Alice.

"We've been through this," Sable replied, waving her hand. "You can't accidentally skewer a bird. No bird would hold still long enough for you to do so."

"Ah." Ruth raised a finger. "But a *stuffed* bird..."

I eyed Ruth. "What are you talking about?"

"I told you, Joseph's a taxidermist," Ruth said, almost reluctantly, like she was afraid to bring it up in front of me again. "What if he was taking care of Casper for Maya and he accidentally killed him somehow? And rather than telling Maya the truth, he replaced Casper with a stuffed cockatiel?"

"And nailed him to his perch and skewered him with a hatpin to give Maya a heart attack?" Sable asked. "If he cared for her at all, he'd never do something like that."

Ruth shrugged. "I was just musing out loud. You're right."

"It would explain why Casper's feet were pinned to his perch, though," I pointed out. "But why use one of Beatrice's hatpins? Beatrice said Joseph wouldn't even kiss her, so it's not like he's out to pin it on Beatrice—pun intended—for denying him or something."

"You're not actually considering this, are you?" Sable asked.

"No, no, now I'm thinking aloud." I scratched my chin and looked to Penny for assistance. "We didn't find blood splatters in the cage."

"*Would* there be blood splatters?" Alice asked. "Wouldn't the pin just kinda...go through?" She made a face.

I looked at Henny, as though she might have the answer. She just cocked her head back at me.

"You may *not* test the theory on Henny," said Penny firmly.

"No, no! Of course not!" I cried.

"It reminds me of a magic trick, like something out of *The Prestige*," Sable said. "The one where they make the dove appear in an empty cage."

"Or vice versa." I nodded in agreement.

Yes, *The Prestige*. A story all about illusion and misdirection. Did Casper's murder have something to do with that?

"I suppose you need to ask yourself, 'What would Tommy and Tuppence do?'" Penny said.

"What would her geese know about anything?" Ruth asked.

"Not her geese, the detectives. From the Agatha Christie novels," Sable corrected.

They continued to talk while I tried to block them from my mind. Penny was right: What would a detective do at this point in the novel? How did he or she sort through all the clues to determine what was a red herring—or illusion—and what was real and true?

We'd started with a bird struck by a hat pin, taxidermy pins and holes in his perch, a bloodless crime scene, and…

I turned to Sable. "Where exactly did you find the grave?"

"It's by the large pond. To the west, near the bench."

"Didn't she have a funeral or something?" Alice asked.

"No, she said she wanted to be alone." I snapped my fingers. "Oh my goodness." I grinned at Penny. "I've got it."

"Really?" they all said at once.

"Yep. I was right all along."

Slings and Sparrows

And on that note, I did what any sensible detective would do in a novel.

I left them to consider my brilliance.

{ 35 }

In Which We Dig A Grave

I did not want to do this.
 I really, really, *really* did not want to do this.
But I was doing it anyway.
I was digging up Casper's grave.
Thankfully, the dirt was still pretty loose from when Maya had buried him almost a week before. It wouldn't take me long, but I still didn't want to do it.

"I feel like we're in *Young Frankenstein*," Penny's voice muttered from beside me in the darkness.

"Could be worse," I said in my best imitation of Igor. "Could be raining."

I half expected the heavens to open and douse us right then and there.

"I promise, I don't intend to bring Casper back to life," I said, pausing in my shoveling. Man, I was out of shape. "He's long past that hope."

Penny wrinkled her nose. "Must we really dig up his body?"

I looked over at her. "Do you really have to ask that question?"

"I just thought I'd check one more time, before it's too late."

I sighed. "I have to. I have to find the truth." I pointed at the small hole. "And the truth lies with his little broken body."

Penny gave a small shiver.

"I can't help thinking of *The Unpleasantness at the Bellona Club* by Dorothy L. Sayers."

"Hmm," was all Penny said.

"If you'll remember: people tried to stop Lord Peter Wimsey from exhuming the body, so he had it done by cover of darkness, just as we are doing now. 'However depressing the thud of earth on the coffin-lid may be, it is music compared to the rattle of gravel and thump of spades which herald a premature and unreverend resurrection.'"

"How do you remember all those quotes?" Penny asked.

I shrugged. "It's a gift."

"One you've always had, by my reckoning. You used to quote complete nursery rhymes out of that Mother Goose book as we played in the crick or climbed on the old slate walls."

"I do look back and wonder at our playing Humpty Dumpty. We might have split our heads open a thousand times falling backward off those walls!"

Penny laughed slightly. "Yes, but somehow we never did." She stared at me as I continued digging. "You do think Casper will be in there, don't you? You don't think we'll dig up the coffin only to find it empty?"

"Or with some other bird's corpse inside?" I suggested. "It would certainly be like a murder mystery novel, wouldn't it?"

"Indeed," said Penny. She chuckled again nervously.

I stopped using the shovel and got down on my knees, digging with my hands. I was worried I'd break through the styrofoam box with the shovel, and that was the last thing I needed.

"Shouldn't we have asked Maya before doing this?" Penny asked.

I grunted. "Little late for that."

"Don't you think Maya will notice?" Penny asked again.

I looked up. "Yes. But I think she'll forgive us if we solve the murder."

Penny pressed her lips together and looked at Henny, who clucked what I took to be a cluck in agreement with me.

"Are you sure this is the right spot?"

I sat back on my knees and rubbed my arm across my forehead, no doubt putting more dirt across my sweaty face. "Are you just going to stand there asking questions or are you going to help?"

"I don't want to get in your way," she murmured.

I shook my head and went back to work. She didn't want to get dirty, that was the true reason.

Neither of us were very good gardeners—I preferred to leave that to people like Sable, who knew what they were doing—but I didn't mind getting a little dirt on my hands every now and then. I had some lovely daffodils, daisies, and tulips that came up every spring. I'd also planted some marigolds around the house in an attempt to keep the deer and cats away. But Penny left all that up to me.

"It's gotta be here someplace," I said. "The marker was right here."

Slings and Sparrows

Penny went over and picked up the lovely wooden cross Joseph had carved. Elegant and simple, it read, "*Casper, friend for life*" in flowing script.

"Are we crazy to get so attached to our birds?" Penny murmured.

My head shot up. "Seriously?"

Penny nodded sadly.

"No crazier than people who name their cars. Cars aren't even alive."

Penny chuckled softly. "True."

My fingernail scraped across something. And it wasn't dirt.

"I've got it!" I yelled, like a kid who'd just uncovered a treasure box.

Now that I knew where to dig, it was only a matter of minutes before I pulled the box out of the dirt and onto my lap.

Penny knelt down beside me and flipped on the small pocket flashlight we'd brought.

"Looks like he had a rough burial," she said, pointing to several nicks in the styrofoam.

"I might have hit it with the shovel accidentally. Good thing I switched to my hands, or I might have gone straight through."

Reverentially, I lifted the lid of the box with that tell-tale squeak of styrofoam.

"Forgive me, Casper," I whispered softly.

It wasn't empty. He was still there, amidst a small collection of dirt. I wondered briefly how anything had managed to get inside.

But then I noticed something more interesting: Casper's body didn't look...dead.

I mean, I hate to get gruesome here for a second—but after all, I did just dig up a grave. So imagine my surprise and the skipping of my heart when I realized his body was not in a state of decomposition...at all. In fact, he still looked as bright and cheery as he had in life.

I screwed up my courage and reached inside the box.

His body was firm. He was stuffed.

I'd been right from the very beginning: we'd been sold a dead parrot.

Casper had never died. Had never been alive to begin with.

Why would someone fake his death?

Only one person could answer that question.

{ 36 }

In Which We Get an Explanation

Penny and I found Maya back at our house, surrounded by piles of packed boxes and suitcases. She looked up with a smile as we stood in the doorway of her bedroom.

"How was the show?" she asked.

Neither of us answered for a moment, each of us waiting for the other to be the first to speak.

"Enlightening," I finally said. "I think you better sit down, Maya."

I motioned to the bed.

Maya tilted her head like a bird. "What's going on? Is something wrong?"

"Yes," said Penny. "We wanted to talk with you, just the three of us."

"About what?" Her eyes wandered to the dirt on the knees of my jeans and hands and face. "Why are you so dirty?"

"We need to talk with you about the murder of Casper," I said, revealing his stuffed body in my hand.

Maya shot up from the edge of the bed, where she'd just sat down.

"Please, sit back down," I said.

She did, slowly and carefully, watching me the way a bird watches a cat.

I took a deep breath. Then I dove in. "I know he's stuffed," I said. "I also know you faked his death. And I know that, inside of him, you've hidden a ruby necklace stolen after your last performance."

Maya's eyes grew wide and her breath stilled.

"What I really want to know is: how long has he been like this?"

Maya looked down at the cockatiel in my hand, then timidly reached forward to take him gently, as if he'd once been a living bird.

"He's been like this as long as I've known him," she said softly. "To me he came alive because I breathed life into him…whistled life into him, I suppose you could say."

"But Casper never sang?" Penny asked softly, her hand resting on Henny.

Maya shook her head. "After my divorce, I dedicated myself to my career as an opera singer. I traveled the circuit and was just beginning to make a name for myself when my voice started to give out. I had developed throat nodules—"

"Like Julie Andrews," I put in.

Maya nodded. "And much like her, the surgery only made things worse. My career was over. I'd lost my singing voice, but

I'd picked up whistling as a sort of work-around. I was wandering an antique store when my eye fell on Casper. He was so lifelike, I jumped when I saw him out of the corner of my eye because I could have sworn he'd moved. When I picked him up, this crazy idea occurred to me: what if I learned to throw my voice like a ventriloquist, in order to make it appear as though this bird were the one whistling? It began as a party trick amongst friends and family. I made changes to him, to make him more like a puppet, so he could move his head and his wings would rise and fall, so he would appear more lifelike."

She set Casper on her hand and showed us. Up close, the movements looked robotic, but on a stage in a big auditorium I could see how she'd gotten away with it.

"One day, we were invited to perform in Philadelphia—one of those friend-of-a-friend type situations. And then before I knew it, we were getting calls to perform all across America. I couldn't believe it. People loved Casper."

Maya sighed. "But they didn't care about me. I was just an old opera singer with a broken set of pipes. No one cared that my voice was slowly coming back. They just wanted to hear Casper whistle. So I had to keep it up." She shrugged. "It was a living."

"But not a very good living," I said. "Or you wouldn't have been tempted to add thievery to your repertoire."

Maya's mouth pressed into a hard line.

"This had nothing to do with Joseph or Beatrice or love triangles or anything like that. It was just about greed. About stolen jewels."

"I did care about Joseph," Maya said passionately, meeting my eyes. "I do care. Why else do you think I'd go to all the trouble of using one of Beatrice's hatpins? I needed him to suspect her, to realize he didn't want her, he wanted *me*." She looked away again. "But you're right. I didn't mean to fall in love with Joseph. That was just a happy accident. I came here originally to hide the ruby necklace."

"From your partner, Billy Bacon," I said.

Maya nodded. "When I discovered Billy had followed me, I was frantic. He knew about the secret compartment in the bottom of Casper's cage. I had to find someplace to hide the necklace where he'd never find it. It suddenly occurred to me that perhaps Casper's stuffed status could be of more use than ever."

He was another Maltese Falcon, just like Ruth's duck with the key.

"So you didn't always hide the jewels you stole inside him?" I asked.

"He's not a purse," Maya scoffed.

Could have fooled me.

"No, we usually hid them in his cage," she continued. "I knew Billy would search there, though, so I had to separate the bird from the cage, just in case."

"But why go to the trouble of faking his murder? Didn't Billy know he was stuffed?"

Maya shook her head. "No one knew. I had to live the lie year-round. I was worried that if I didn't, someone would discover the truth. I could never let anyone get a really good look."

"Sounds lonely," I said. "I can't imagine living alone with only a stuffed bird for company, always trying to hide the truth."

Slings and Sparrows

Maya kept her focus on Casper. "Moving here, making friends, letting myself learn to be a part of other people's lives again, meeting Joseph...it's been different."

"Good different?"

"Yeah." Maya gave a soft smile.

It was like the magician known as "Ching Ling Fu" in *The Prestige*, who spent every day shuffling around like an old man, when in reality he was fit and healthy. In this way he'd hidden the fact that for his one great trick, revealing a large goldfish bowl full of live fish from nowhere, it was actually carried between his legs.

In the two months since Casper moved in, I'd never once seen him flying, even in the sunroom. If I'd glimpsed him standing there in his cage, I'd thought him proud and haughty. Then Maya would quickly cover him because he needed "sleep."

Why hadn't I caught on sooner that I had a real-life magician living in my own house?

"I knew that if Bacon stole the cage with Casper in it," Maya continued, "he'd realize Casper was stuffed and...dig the necklace out of him, especially if he couldn't find the necklace where it was usually hidden."

I recalled the loose dirt I'd found inside Casper's box, and the nicks on the outside of his styrofoam coffin.

"I think after he broke in to search the cage and didn't find anything, he actually did get as far as thinking you'd buried the jewels with Casper's body," I said, "but it never occurred to him you'd actually hide them *inside* Casper."

Maya grimaced. "I didn't think I'd ever go so far as that, either."

"What was the next part of your plan?" Penny asked. "Were you just going to cut your losses and leave Casper buried with the necklace inside him?"

"Of course not." She looked sadly at the bird in her hands. "I was going to dig him up and retrieve the necklace on my way out of town."

"And hope that this time Billy wouldn't find you?"

Maya shrugged slightly. "Yes."

Penny shook her head. "I don't think Billy will ever give up. Is it really worth it?"

Maya focused on Penny. "Half a million dollars? Yes, I think it's worth it—wouldn't you?"

Penny pursed her lips and patted Henny. "No," she said.

Maya snorted and looked at me as if to say, "Do you believe this?"

"I don't think it's worth it, either," I said. "You'll be on the run for the rest of your life. How far do you think Bacon would go to get that necklace from you? What if next time it's your own life that's at risk and not a stuffed bird's?"

Maya scoffed. "You two are nuts." She wrapped her hand tightly around Casper and turned as though to place him in a bag.

I put my hand firmly on her arm.

She looked up at me.

I shook my head sadly. "I'm sorry, Maya. I can't let you take that necklace."

Maya's jaw tightened, and for just a moment I wondered how far *she'd* go for half a million dollars.

Then the tension slowly released from her face and she crumpled back onto the edge of the bed, holding out the cockatiel's body.

"Take him," she said. "I don't deserve him."

Penny gave Maya a small pat on the shoulder before gently removing Casper and making her way toward the door.

I let go of Maya's arm.

"What will you do with me?" Maya asked softly. I realized she was speaking through tears.

I looked at Penny.

"We'll mail the necklace to the police in D.C. anonymously," she said. "Let them return it to its rightful owner. Once Billy hears about it, he'll stop chasing you, since he'll know you haven't got it."

I smiled in agreement. I couldn't have thought of a more beautiful plan.

Maya looked up. She'd definitely been crying. "Really? You're not going to turn me in?"

"For what? Faking the murder of your own bird?" I laughed. "And the necklace will be returned, so all's well that ends well, as they say."

Penny gave Maya a comforting smile.

"Can you show us?" Penny asked quietly.

"Show you?" Maya asked.

"Could you show us how you whistle without moving your lips?" Penny held out Casper, upright, as though he were preparing for his final performance.

Maya studied Casper. And then, all of a sudden, Casper began to *sing*.

He whistled "Edelweiss" from *The Sound of Music*, and I admit, I began to cry.

"How do you do it?" Penny asked, shaking her head in amazement.

Maya hesitated. "It's sort of like beatboxing. I whistle from my throat, and let just a little bit of air through my teeth. If anyone watched my throat closely, they would see it moving and know the truth immediately."

"You need to reveal that truth, Maya," Penny said.

Maya grimly focused on her cockatiel. "No one would be interested in this."

"What are you talking about?" I couldn't believe it. "What you and Casper used to do, it's all the more incredible because not only were you whistling, you were also distracting your audience with a stuffed bird. It's the art of misdirection. Besides, how many whistling ventriloquists are out there?"

Maya smiled.

"People love ventriloquists, don't they? They know the puppet isn't real, but they still enjoy the dialogue—or monologue?—all the while wondering how you, the performer, have given a puppet such personality," Penny encouraged. "Your whistling is so beautiful, I think people would enjoy it even knowing the truth. People would love to hear your story and see you whistle with a new bird, or any puppet for that matter."

"It's truly something unique, Maya," I agreed with a smile. "Embrace it!"

"You really think so?" She looked from Penny to me, then back to Casper.

"Yes," Penny and I said in unison, and Henny gave a small cluck in endorsement.

"You two are really something." Maya shook her head and wiped the back of her hand across her wet eyes.

I looked at my sister. "Just another day for the Old Bird Society."

Epilogue

The day Maya left, the goodbyes were quick and terse. Alice offered her card, but Maya waved it away. Penny and I gave her a hug, but no one else even proffered a farewell shake of the hand. We were all happy to see the problem leaving, though I did wish Maya the best of luck on her new career path. I hoped she'd learned her lesson, and wouldn't find herself lifting the odd piece of jewelry anymore.

Beatrice and I had made up after she learned Penny and I had been right about Billy Bacon. There'd been no I-told-you-so's, only apologies, hugs, and some tears.

As I looked around our circle of friends, I wondered if anyone else had a dark secret of which I was unaware. I certainly hoped not. I, for one, had experienced enough mystery for a lifetime.

But it was only a few days later, after I'd pushed my library books into the book drop, that I turned and found myself face-to-face with a small, round woman wearing thick glasses that magnified her eyes to the size of an owl's.

"Excuse me, but are you Ms. Fulton?" she asked in a slight Pittsburgh accent, barely above a whisper.

Slings and Sparrows

I looked around before realizing she was talking to me. "Me?" I said, a hand to my chest. "Yes, I suppose I am. But please, call me Goose."

The woman's eyes got even rounder. "Goose?"

"Yes. What can I do for you?"

She glanced from side to side. "I don't mean to be nebby, but I'm looking for a place to live. I just finished the best hoagie I've ever had this side of Pittsburgh—"

"Ah, yes." I gave her a wink. "The Bogie Hoagie."

"Yes! Humphrey Bogart was simply a dream, so I just had to try it! Anyway, the nice owner of the Quaint Quail said yinz had bird-friendly living arrangements and I thought I might inquire."

I smiled. Good old Aunt Connie had already found us a replacement. "You've come to the right place. What kind of bird do you have?"

"She's a tawny frogmouth."

"A what?"

"A tawny frogmouth. Looks like an owl, sounds like an owl, but isn't an owl. She's very sweet, very quiet, and is excellent at a game of hide and seek. I'll only have her for a short while," the little woman said softly, pushing her glasses up her nose. "I'm rehabilitating her."

I raised my brows. I wasn't certain what that had to do with anything, but the woman looked tame enough.

Then again...

"I'd love to meet her, but we'll need to run a background check first."

PATRICIA MEREDITH

THE END

Recipes

Much Ado About Muffins

Ingredients:

½ C butter
⅔ C sugar + ¼ C sugar
1 ⅓ C flour
½ tsp salt
½ tsp cinnamon
½ tsp nutmeg
2 tsp baking powder
1 tsp lemon zest
2 eggs
½ C milk
½ C pistachios, blended finely + ¼ C pistachios, chopped
1 tsp almond extract
1 tsp vanilla extract
Green food coloring

Directions:

1. Preheat oven to 425°F.
2. Place muffin liners into two 12-count muffin tins.
3. In a stand mixer, cream the butter and ⅔ C sugar.
4. In a separate bowl, combine flour, salt, cinnamon, nutmeg, and baking powder. Stir till mixed.
5. Pour flour mixture into stand-mixer and combine. Add lemon zest, eggs, and milk. Finally add the finely blended pistachios, keeping to the side the chopped pistachios.
6. Add almond and vanilla extract. Drop in green food coloring until mixture is your desired color.
7. Scoop batter into each prepared muffin tin. Mix ¼ C sugar with chopped pistachios in small bowl. Sprinkle over tops of muffins.
8. Bake at 425°F for 15-20 minutes. Enjoy plain or with a little butter.

Brothers Carrot-mazov

Ingredients:

1 lb. carrots
4 T butter
2 T honey
1 T thyme, rosemary, or both
Salt and pepper to taste

Directions:

1. Shave and slice carrots.
2. Place on stovetop in a large pot with enough water to cover and a pinch of salt. Boil for about 10 minutes until crisp-tender.
3. Drain and remove from pot.
4. In same pan, combine remaining ingredients. Cook over medium heat about 2 minutes.
5. Return carrots to pot.
6. Cook and stir until fully glazed and the carrots are your desired tenderness.
7. Season to taste with salt and pepper. Serve hot with your favorite meal.

Acknowledgements

This book was made possible by the help of many dedicated friends and family.

First and foremost, I'd like to thank Mike and Linda Chase, to whom this book is dedicated. Thank you for inviting us into the comfort of your homestead and hearts, filling our lives with hours of play amongst trees of plum, peach, apple, and pear, chasing the peacocks off our lettuces but then teaching us to thank them for eating all the slugs, walking down the long, winding country roads to watch the sun set over the wheat fields, and opening our eyes to the hard work and dedication it takes to keep sheep, chickens, ducks, peacocks, guinea fowl, and more happy and chirping. May God bless you and keep you.

To my Lord and Savior, from whom and by whom all words flow, even the funny ones.

My husband, Andrew, for his never-ending encouragement, love, and laughter. My kids, who will never know how lucky they were to spend so many lovely years on the farm.

My parents and parents-in-law, who have blessed me with so much encouragement, prayer, and support.

To my editor, Corin Fayé, who eagerly anticipates anything I send him, even the ones that are a bit more crazy.

My amazing team of Beta Readers: Noelle Austin, Kathy Buckmaster, Anne Fischer, Diane Gordon, Brenda McCosby, Maggie Meredith, Renae Meredith, Su Meredith, Lydia Pierce, Sarah Pounder, Julie Rizzo, Catie Rizzo, Jessie Rizzo, Dean Rizzo, Sue Rizzo, Beth Sanchez, Kathleen Sharp, Nicole Wagner, Susan Walker, and Rebecca Writz.

And you, dear Reader. Thank you for taking the time to read this book! Would you please leave me a review so I know how much you loved it?

If you'd like to learn more about our life on the farm, the historical '90s, and to find delicious recipes, be sure to visit my website at Patricia-Meredith.com, my YouTube channel @pmeredithauthor, and follow me on social media as @pmeredithauthor.

Thank you for reading!

Patricia Meredith is an author of historical and cozy mysteries. When she's not writing, she's playing board games with her husband, creating imaginary worlds with her two children, or out in the garden reading a good book with a cup of tea.

For all the latest updates, you can follow her as @pmeredithauthor on YouTube, Goodreads, Instagram, and Facebook, and sign up for her newsletter at Patricia-Meredith.com.